THE BLACK

# THE GUARDIANS OF SIN

# JONATHAN L. FERRARA

Dragonwell Publishing

# CONTENTS

To my dad for giving up his dreams
so that my brother and I could fulfill our own.
To my mom for telling me I can be whatever I want.
To Samantha Blackburn
for spending so many nights reading about Demonio.
Most of all, to Aaron Ferrara,
whose heart, like mine, is in this story.

 INNOCENCE

[As I walk through the valley of the shadow of
death, I shall fear no evil, for you are with me;
your rod and your staff, they comfort me.]

*Psalm 23:4*

The dark night engulfed Nicholas. His sweaty palms trembled against his thighs as he stood in the valley, knowing there was a good chance he was about to die. His throat tightened, as he imagined all the terrible things that could be happening to Amy. What if she was hurt? What if she wasn't even alive? By now, Nicholas had an open mind to the impossible. Anything could happen. Nothing was off limits.

Fog dripped down the valley walls and rolled past his feet. The hazy air made it difficult to see, until a spark of ember shone in the distance. Decrepit gravestones scattered across the dead field, stopping at the end of the valley at a palace of white stone. Enticed by curiosity, Nicholas made his way through the valley. Thin brittle bones crunched under his feet as he continued on. A group of limp, old men crept behind, dragging toward him. Their hands and arms swayed like a rag doll's as they lurched through the fog. The men cried, grinding their teeth with pain, as though they had been waiting centuries for this moment, for Nicholas's arrival.

Nicholas halted at the entrance of the palace, eyes locked on the elegant script etched along the front doors: *Blackwell Manor*. Cold air scraped his skin and reached down his dry throat like a claw. His breathing became harsh as he stared at his family's name. His trembling hand slid into his back pocket, fingers fighting for his inhaler. Quickly he placed it against his lips.

A cold, hollow voice echoed across the valley, chilling him to his very core. The words hung in the air: *I know a secret that could change the world.*

Nicholas calmed his nerves with a puff from his inhaler. How could he, a boy, have come this far and survived so much? It seemed as if Nicholas had forgotten a lot in his walk through the valley, as if his mind was erased in such a short period of time. He had completely forgotten how he got to the Valley of Death, why he held six random objects in his backpack and what had happened to his friend. There wasn't too much he could recall, but one thing was certain: he was about to face the greatest evil imaginable.

As he opened the front doors of the Blackwell Manor, he stared into the most beautiful blue eyes he had ever seen. And then he remembered…

The snowfall had stopped and thick ruby curtains fell together, making the stage disappear like a magic act. Seven-year-old Nicholas Blackwell followed his parents' lead and stood between them to applaud. He looked up at his mother, who had the same smile on her face as when the show began. Her dark red hair was elegantly done up, and her long black dress sparkled as the overhead lights beamed from the stage. He then looked to his father who towered over him, wearing an exquisite black suit with a blue tie to match his eyes. Oliver continued to clap, and Nicholas did the same.

It was the largest theater in New York City, and Nicholas had a hard time weaving through the tall masses of lavishly dressed people. He tried to keep up with his parents, but one wrong turn lead him to an unfamiliar hall, where he halted at a ferocious gargoyle statue. He searched frantically for his parents through the sea of people, standing on the base of the marble statue to get a better look. His chest tightened with every second that went by, and as he reached for his inhaler, he completely forgot that he had given it to his mother to hold in her purse.

An enormous gloved hand rested on Nicholas's shoulder, and he turned to see a giant of a man hovering over him.

"Hey there Nicholas, you alright?" the man said in a thick, burly voice.

Nicholas tried to respond but couldn't find words. The man reached into his coat pocket, and Nicholas took this opportunity to run into the crowd. The man yelled for Nicholas to return, but as he tried to follow, his coat caught on the teeth of the gargoyle.

Nicholas surged through the crowd, feeling as though he could faint at any moment. His vision blurred as he felt dizzy. Just as he felt he would topple over, he saw red hair and his mother's arms stretching toward him.

"Nicholas!" Kathleen shouted in relief as she pulled the inhaler from her purse.

"Sorry," Nicholas said from behind his inhaler.

Oliver put a hand on his shoulder. "You scared us to death."

Nicholas looked up. "There was a man, he knew my name."

His parents exchanged a worried glance.

After an unsettling moment, Oliver knelt down to be level with his son. "Nicholas, I want you to promise me you will stay by our side, alright?"

Nicholas nodded and looked to his mother, who had not taken her eyes from him since they had found him.

In the lobby, Mr. and Mrs. Blackwell mingled with some friends, colleagues and one of Kathleen's old professors from New York University. Nicholas made a round of introductions with his parents' friends. He counted five pinches to the cheek, three "look how tall you've gotten" and two "you look just like your father". He quickly forgot faces as he was being introduced to an endless stream of people and hid behind his father, arms wrapped around Oliver's leg.

"Oliver," said a man with a thick mustache and a cane, looking as though he had just stepped out of an old Hollywood film, "How goes the Blackwell Foundation?"

"Very well, thank you," Oliver said proudly. "This year, the hospital is looking brighter than ever with over two dozen volunteers for Christmas. The donations have been most generous, the best I've ever seen. The children will have a truly blessed Christmas this year."

"Good to hear," the man said, leaning against his cane. "Remind me to contribute a little extra." He winked and turned to Oliver's wife. "Kathleen, may I say you look enchanting this evening?"

"Thank you, Professor Larson."

"I hear you've taken over the homeless shelter down on 32nd street. How is it holding up?"

"It'll be a Christmas to remember." Kathleen's contagious smile had everyone joining in.

Professor Larson now looked to Nicholas. "Nicholas Blackwell, I presume?"

Nicholas nodded as he came out from behind his father.

"It's very nice to finally meet you. I've heard wonderful things. Your parents just beam about you. You know, you look just like your father."

Three times. That was the third time Nicholas had been compared to his father.

It was getting late when Nicholas's parents finally said goodbye to their friends. It was one of the only nights Nicholas was allowed to stay up so late—a holiday treat. He loved it. Staying up late made him feel grown up.

Out on the street Oliver waved down a taxi. Nicholas got a glimpse of his father's ring embedded with an amethyst stone. A family heirloom, one that had been around for many generations. Not too long ago, Oliver said that one day the ring would be handed down to Nicholas. Ever since, he had appreciated the ring much more.

The taxi made its way toward their home through the labyrinth of a city toward the Upper East Side. The city was lit up, busier than ever on the Christmas Eve, and the shops stayed open long past midnight. When they arrived, Kathleen helped Nicholas out of the car as Oliver paid the taxi driver, giving him a generous tip that made the man beam with gratitude, thanking him over and over again.

"Happy Holidays to you and your family. Take care," Oliver said.

"You as well, Mr. Blackwell. God bless." The taxi driver waved goodbye and drove off into the night, probably heading back home early, now that he had made more than enough in tips to make his shift worthwhile.

Huddled under her cozy jacket, Kathleen wrapped her arms around Nicholas. Her warmth overpowered the bitter cold night. "You know Nicholas, Santa Claus is probably already delivering toys to children around the world."

"He is, isn't he?" Nicholas jumped with excitement. "I can hardly wait until morning."

"Me too." She smiled.

Oliver joined his family at the front door and took out his house key from his coat pocket. Just as he unlocked the door, his cell phone rang. Kathleen's look made him hesitate.

"It'll just take a minute," he assured her.

"Alright, but remember it's our night." She took Nicholas's hand and led him up the stairs to his bedroom. She helped him change out of his suit. He took it off reluctantly. He loved dressing up like his father.

In his pajamas, Nicholas knelt down beside his bed. He wrapped his hands together and closed his eyes. "Now I lay me down to sleep, I pray the Lord my soul to keep. If I die before I wake, I pray the Lord my soul to take."

Kathleen smiled warmly as she watched her son pray.

"Dear God, I pray that everyone in the entire world has a great Christmas and has someone to share it with. Thank you for my mommy and daddy and everything. I love you God. Goodnight."

Nicholas jumped into bed and crawled under his thick, superhero-themed comforter. Kathleen gave him Dexter, his stuffed bear, and kissed him on the cheek, then turned the bedroom lights off, leaving a nightlight on in the corner of his room.

"Goodnight mommy."

"Goodnight sweetheart. I love you." She closed the door behind her, leaving it open just a crack. Nicholas hugged Dexter and closed his eyes. It didn't take long at all before he dozed off.

The sound of shattering glass awoke Nicholas. He looked at his bedside clock. 3:33. Muffled voices echoed from downstairs. He pushed off his comforter and crept toward the door. Through the crack in the doorway, he could see that the light in the living room was on. The unfamiliar voices grew louder. Trying to move as quietly as he could, he tiptoed toward the edge of the staircase and slipped his head between the rails of the banister to get a better view.

His heart raced as a man came into view. The same huge man with black gloves he'd seen by the gargoyle statue in the theatre was now standing in his living room.

"Alright Blackwells, where are you hiding them?" The man moved aside, revealing Oliver and Kathleen, bound to chairs. Nicholas covered his mouth to stifle a gasp. Now that the man faced Nicholas's direction, he could see what the man had been hiding under his coat. Though he looked human, his skin had an odd green tint. Scars showed through his thick facial hair.

Nicholas also saw another man, more stout than tall, stuffing his mouth with cookies. His jaw seemed to unhinge as he fit in piles of cookies with ease.

"Would you stop filling your face and get over here?!" The big man in the coat smacked his companion on the back and a whole cookie flew from his mouth and crumbled on the floor.

"Sorry, Mr. Romulus, sir."

Romulus turned back to face the Blackwells. "I'm only going to ask you one more time, Mr. and Mrs. Blackwell. Where are the sins?" He circled them in long, stalking steps.

"We have no idea what you're talking about," Oliver spoke weakly.

The man swung, hitting Oliver in the face. A tooth flew out of his mouth. The man eating cookies laughed, crumbs falling down the front of his overalls, his enormous belly bouncing with each menacing chuckle.

"Oliver, Oliver, Oliver," Romulus taunted. "Why do you make me hurt you?" He stopped his pacing and leaned into Oliver, then glanced at Kathleen quivering in her chair, her dress tattered, her tangled hair half-covering her face. "You think I don't know the famous Blackwells? You Oliver, the infamous Seeker who had sent so many of my kind back to Hell." He turned sharply to Kathleen. "And your wife, Kathleen Blackwell formerly known as Kathleen LaGuardia. Studied at New York

University where she majored in Philosophy and Religion with a minor in Demonology," he smirked, leaning closer. "Your beauty could bring the Guardian of Envy to tears."

"We do not Seek anymore," Kathleen said, fighting to speak through a cut lip.

"And why was that, again? Was it because you finally were able to conceive?" He pressed his hand against her belly.

"Don't touch her!" Oliver bellowed.

The man with the cookies laughed louder.

Again Oliver was smacked across the face. "Where are the sins, Oliver?! Where are they?!" Romulus cut Oliver's ropes and forced him out of the chair, pushing him against the glossy, wooden floorboards kicking him three times in the stomach.

"Stop it, please!" Kathleen cried.

Romulus pulled out a pistol from his side pocket and shoved it into Oliver's face.

Nicholas's heart pounded so hard that he was sure his chest would burst. Breathing became difficult.

"I'm gonna ask you one more time, Kathleen, or your husband will die. Where are the sins?" Romulus demanded, as he tightened his grip on the pistol.

"If I tell you the whereabouts of the sins, you'll just kill us anyway." Tears fell hard down Kathleen's face.

"Ah, Katie… Can I call you Katie?" his voice softened, but Kathleen didn't answer. "I am a man of my word. Tell me where you hid them and all of this will go away."

"Kathleen, don't," Oliver said.

"Shut up!" Romulus's face reddened, distended veins pulsing beneath his skin. He shook the pistol. "I will pull this trigger. Now answer me, Kathleen! Where are you hiding the sins?"

"They are contained."

"Where?"

"Sins can only be contained within… innocence." As the words left her lips, Oliver closed his eyes and muttered the word 'no' over and over again.

"Innocence," Romulus smirked. "A child. You brilliant woman. Now, how come we never thought of that?" He turned to his friend who had finished the Christmas cookies. "I love it. Simple, yet righteous. Innocence, all a part of the great Divine." He looked up to the ceiling, as if it was to the Heavens.

Nicholas quickly leaned back from the banister so that he couldn't be spotted. Then he heard the most horrible sound. A gun shot. Kathleen screamed.

Nicholas looked back downstairs. He couldn't see his father behind the couch. Kathleen hung her head and sunk into her chair as low as the ropes would allow her.

"You evil son of a bitch!"

"Ouch, Katie. There is no need for all that." Romulus lifted her chin and looked straight into her eyes with a menacing smirk.

"You said you wouldn't hurt him."

"Hurt him?" Romulus gave a slight chuckle. "No, I didn't hurt him. I freed him. You should be thanking me. I thought the Blackwells were all about protecting the Divine. Now he is at peace."

Kathleen spat in his face. With the sleeve of his shirt he mopped his face clean.

"You shouldn't have done that," he said, hands leaning against the arms of her chair. "You see, Katie, we've been watching your family for a very long time now. And I know for a fact that when you and your husband fought the Guardians of Sin and contained them, like you so honorably admit, that you were actually… pregnant."

Her face was now soaked with tears. She shook her head, begging for him to stop.

"Now I can't think of anything more innocent than a child that hasn't even been born. A child that hasn't even had a chance to sin." He turned to the man covered in cookie crumbs. "Get the boy."

"No!" she screamed.

Nicholas jumped to his feet and hurried up to the third level to his parents' bedroom. He didn't care how much noise he made, he just knew he had to hurry. He hadn't even realized he was carrying Dexter until he ran into the bedroom. Just as he crawled under the bed he heard the sound of another gunshot and his mother's screams stopped.

# ST. CHRISTOPHER'S ACADEMY

He could have puked right then, but the fear of the man following him kept Nicholas focusing on other things. It hadn't occurred to him yet that he had just become an orphan.

Nicholas hugged Dexter tightly as he lay under the bed. He tugged the silk sheets so they fell to the floor, hiding him, but he could still make out the silhouette of the dresser and the bedroom door. By now he became aware of his harsh wheezing. His asthma was always his crutch, holding him back from running, riding a bike, or even playing in the snow. And now it was going to get him caught and perhaps murdered. *Where is my inhaler? Oh yeah, my bathroom drawer. There have to be more. Mom got a lot and put them in different places. Where are they? In the kitchen junk drawer. The glove compartment in the car. There was one near my stack of video games, in my backpack. Ms. Brown had one in the classroom, but there had to be more.*

His chest was about to explode. *Mom had one in her nightstand!* Nicholas jumped out from underneath the bed and pulled open the drawer. He felt faint as he grabbed the inhaler and took a puff, counted twenty seconds and then repeated. But the usual relief wasn't fast enough. He felt dizzy as he staggered forward, leaning against the mattress to catch his fall.

Right before he could dive back to his hiding place, the bedroom door swung open. He could have sworn it was his mother, running toward him. He caught a glimpse of her auburn hair. His vision went blurry, and then darkness.

By the time he woke up, it was Christmas morning. He didn't get to run into his parents' bedroom. He wasn't opening presents or drinking eggnog. This Christmas morning, Nicholas Blackwell woke up in a hospital bed.

A nurse came in and tried to explain to Nicholas what had happened. As she spoke, Nicholas let his mind wander. He did not want to hear what she was saying. She was skirting the facts, sugarcoating them, but he knew the truth. His parents were murdered. He had seen it with his own eyes.

"How did I get here?" Nicholas asked.

"No one knows," she answered. "You were found in the lobby, passed out on the floor. One minute the lobby was empty and the next you were there. Looks like you've got a guardian angel on your side."

"But if I just appeared, how did you know what happened to my parents?" Nicholas asked.

And then she grinned. It was a smile of pure evil. Her teeth darkened and her face cracked with wrinkles. Her hair unclipped from a bun and fell down her face in thick cords. She grabbed Nicholas by his wrist and pulled him closer. Her body trembled as she sniffed up and down his arm like a hound dog hunting for a clue. He tried pulling away, but her grip was too strong.

"Where are you hiding them?" she demanded.

"I'm not hiding anything!"

"I smell them on you." Her teeth bit down against her bottom lip. Her now-yellow eyes gazed into Nicholas's. "Your blood will be spilled so they will be resurrected and regain their power over the Mankind's World. Do not mistake it, the seven great Princes will once again wear their Crowns."

"Let go of me." Nicholas tried harder to pull free.

The door swung open and a man stepped into the room. His long, black robe flapped against his black leather shoes as he stood in the frame of the doorway. The upturned stiff white collar around his neck identified him as a man of the church.

The nurse smirked at Nicholas before disappearing into a cloud of ash.

The priest rushed to Nicholas, handing him an inhaler. Nicholas hadn't even realized that he was losing his breath until he puffed the medicine into his constricting lungs.

"Did she harm you?" the priest asked.

He shook his head, unable to say a word as he felt his airways start to open again. The scene with the nurse repeated in his head. *People don't just disappear.*

"Good. My name is Father Henry. I worked with your parents for many years. In accordance with their wishes you are now in the protection of the Vatican."

"What's the Vatican?" Nicholas said, finding trouble sounding out the name.

"It is the highest authority of the Catholic church." Father Henry took off Nicholas's blanket and helped him out of bed. "I have already checked you out of the hospital. We mustn't waste time. The plane leaves in less than two hours." He glanced at his wristwatch.

"What plane?"

"To England. There is a private boarding school there, not too far from London, in the forest of Epping. It is a safe place for you, the only safe place left."

"But I don't want to go to England. I want to go home," Nicholas said, ready to cry.

The priest placed his hand on Nicholas's shoulder. "I'm sorry, Nicholas, but you don't have a choice. Your life is in terrible danger as long as you are here. Now we mustn't waste any more time."

He took Nicholas into the hallway. Nurses strolled past them and Nicholas wanted to scream for help, but he no longer trusted nurses. They sped through the lobby as the front door to the emergency room automatically opened. A black limousine waited beside two ambulances. Father Henry opened the limo door and they both scooted in. Once the door shut, the limo pulled out from its parking spot.

Nicholas kept his eyes on the road ahead. "My parents are really dead."

"The only ones that die are the ones we forget," the priest said softly.

"What about the funeral? Aren't my parents going to have a funeral?" Nicholas had only been to one funeral before. His Great Aunt Carolyn on his mother's side. He knew his parents would need one as well.

"Of course. But you cannot go. They will expect you there," he answered.

"Who will expect me there?"

The priest didn't answer.

The rest of the car ride was silent. Nicholas was given a suitcase of new things. He zipped it open but it revealed nothing exciting, just clothes and a passport. No toys or games. Not even a picture of his parents. He wasn't sure why none of his things were packed, including Dexter. He so badly wanted to go back home and grab some of his belongings, but he knew what the priest's answer would be.

"Who are you?" Nicholas turned to the priest.

"I am the Dean of the academy, which you will be attending. Your new home."

"How come my parents never said anything about you?" Nicholas asked.

Father Henry's bushy white eyebrows raised as he turned to face Nicholas. "Your parents didn't tell you everything, you know. Parents rarely do."

Nicholas could feel the priest's cold demeanor, as though dealing with a little boy was an inconvenience. Not wanting to be any more of a bother, Nicholas rested his head against the cold glass window and drifted off to sleep.

The car ride was not a smooth one, and felt like a theme park attraction. Nicholas jerked awake. He tried forgetting the last twenty-four hours, but every time he fell asleep he dreamed of his parents being shot. There was no controlling the grim reminder that his parents were gone. Not even the plane ride could distract him. It had only left Nicholas with more time to soak in the terrible loss and come to terms with the idea of being an orphan.

Nicholas looked outside for the first time since they had landed in England. There was hardly any civilization in Epping Forest besides rare cottages and bed-and-breakfasts. They continued their drive, venturing deeper through the forest, vanishing within the sea of tall trees.

The car turned onto a new road and stopped abruptly. Nicholas peeked out of the window to see an iron gate, tall and broad, with gargoyle statues on the gateposts leering down at him. He threw himself back into his seat as the gates pulled open and the driver continued on toward an enormous red brick estate.

"This is it?" Nicholas asked, looking at the wide structure that seemed to have no end.

The sheet of black glass in front of him lowered to reveal the back of the driver's head. "Sure is, Mr. Blackwell. Welcome to St. Christopher's Academy."

Father Henry gestured for Nicholas to open the door and step out.

A nun was waiting for them at the doorstep. She was a heavier woman with curly gray hair framing her chubby face. Her eyes glistened as she stepped toward Nicholas. "You poor thing. I am Sister Margaret. Let me show you to your new room." She took him by the shoulders and guided him inside.

The entrance was beautiful. The floor was made of marble and abstract artwork lined the hall. Nicholas followed the nun up an elegant staircase to the second floor and on to the dormitories in the west wing. As she walked, Sister Margaret kept talking, explaining to him about the school. Nicholas learned that the school was filled with hundreds of students from around the world and that the hallways were never usually this quiet.

The nun approached a room at the far end of the hallway and flung the door open. Nicholas looked inside.

The room was pathetically small and dull, its floor covered with an ugly blue carpet that matched the thin window drapes. Two narrow beds occupied the opposite sides of the room. A desk between the beds held the most ancient computer and monitor screen Nicholas had ever seen. But then he spotted something that made his heart race, something he thought he would never see again. Dexter, his stuffed bear, was laying against the pillow on one of the beds. Nicholas hurried to him and grabbed Dexter, the last bit of home he had left.

"Merry Christmas, Nicholas." Sister Margaret smiled from the doorway.

She left Nicholas alone to adjust to his new room, but it would be a very long time before he would start to feel comfortable in his new home.

 # THE NEW GIRL AT SCHOOL

Å man appeared out of nowhere, walking along the school building, making his way through the wet grass. The new moon sat above him like a smile in the sky, as though someone in the Heavens thought the night a curious one. Fog rolled toward the gate, stopping at its bars as if aware that the gargoyle statues at the gate entrance would not allow passage.

The cool night air brushed gently across Gabriel's face as he started toward the gate, picking his way through the dark forest. His purpose was much too important to delay any longer. There was no time even to change out of his janitor uniform.

He waited.

An old serpent pushed its way through the fog, slithering across the grass. Only the gate stood between Gabriel and the snake. The serpent rose out of the fog, its body twisted in the grass as its huge head swung toward Gabriel, hissing.

"You are not welcome here," Gabriel said with more power in his voice than he normally cared to use. "Leave this place and never come back!"

"*Do not mistake it, Gabriel, whether it be tonight, or years from now, I will taste his blood.*" A forked tongue slid out from the serpent's thin mouth.

"It is the will of our Father."

"*I have no Father!*" the serpent hissed. "*And you, my brother, are nothing more than His puppet.*"

"As long as I stay within these gates, my light becomes this school's haven, which means you are not allowed to cross here, understood?"

The serpent smirked. "*Every light goes out, even yours, brother. Our epic battle might have been fought eons ago, but I will have my revenge, and my vengeance starts with that boy. You can't stay there forever. I will not rest until the Guardians have reawakened.*" The serpent's head hit the grass and it slithered on into the woods.

It was nine years later and the summer was coming to an end. Autumn was quickly approaching, filling the woods that circled St. Christopher's Academy with auburn leaves. The days were already becoming cooler, with a gentle breeze that welcomed the students to the new year.

Nicholas awoke in darkness. He pulled his pillow off his head and tossed it aside. His tired hand rose, fingers fighting for the dangling chain nearby. He tugged it and the blinds opened, letting the sunlight into his room, its flood waking him up faster than an alarm clock. Nicholas forced himself out of bed and stretched. Running his fingers through his thick black hair, he stared out of the window at the kids arriving at school. A smile spread across his face.

Most kids Nicholas's age dreaded the end of summer break because it meant goodbye to late nights, sleeping in and just simply being lazy. It meant a farewell to freedom and the return to reading, writing, and arithmetics. But for Nicholas, the end of summer break meant the end of being alone. He was, after all, the only student at St. Christopher's Academy who lived in the dormitory all year round. During the holidays and summer break, he had nowhere else to go. Even the nuns and Father Henry would leave the school grounds every once in awhile. But not Nicholas. This school was the only home he had, he had never ventured out, so he was ecstatic to have familiar faces around the school again after three months of playing card games and chess matches with Sister Margaret.

Nicholas pulled a white t-shirt over his head and forced his feet into a pair of shoes. He frantically ran around his room, collecting all his laundry that was scattered; a sock on the nightstand, shirts under his bed, a pair of jeans hanging from the heater, and a jacket over his lampshade. If Sister Margaret was to see his room the way it was on the day students were returning to school, he would probably be stuck helping in the cafeteria for a week. Besides, today was the day he got a new roommate. The new kid needed somewhere to put his things.

Just as Nicholas began clearing a drawer in the dresser, he heard a knock on his bedroom door. He panicked. It could be Sister Margaret. He quickly made his bed and hid Dexter under a pillow, just as the door opened.

A woman entered. She was tall, lean, and beautiful, with platinum blonde hair that followed the angles of her face. The boy coming behind her was her complete opposite—short and tubby, with glasses as round as his face falling down to the tip of his nose. Her son? Nicholas frowned, watching the newcomers.

"This must be your new roommate," the woman said to the boy.

Nicholas smiled. "Nice to meet you. I'm Nicholas."

"Pleased to make your acquaintance," the tubby boy said nasally. "My name is Theodore Fink."

*Fink?* That didn't sound like an actual name. Besides, what kind of a person talked like this, as if reciting a 19th century novel?

A man—probably Theodore's dad—entered the room lugging three suitcases, while holding a cell phone between his shoulder and cheek. He dropped the suitcases on the empty bed. "This is a nice place… No, no, not you," he said into the phone. "Julia is worth more than that. This new film is going to put her on the *top* of every agent's 'A' list. Guaranteed!"

His mom gave Theodore a kiss on the cheek, leaving a stain of her glossy pink lipstick behind. Normal sixteen-year-olds would have been embarrassed by the kiss, especially in front of strangers, but Theodore didn't seem bothered by it.

"We'll let you boys get to know each other," the woman said. "We really have to catch our flight. We're flying straight to Egypt for the next film."

"You're an actress?" Nicholas asked.

"Yes." She looked at him with curiosity, as if surprised he hadn't recognized her. "I'm Julia Fink. You probably remember me from *Little Miss Millionaire* or *The Haunted State*. Oh, and my most recent film, *The Last Crime of Charles Dotson*. It was a box office explosion." Her eyelids fluttered.

"Of course," Nicholas said politely. He had never heard of any of those movies. She did look familiar, though—probably from a magazine he'd seen somewhere. When Sister Margaret left the academy, she always brought him back a handful of magazines to keep him in touch with the outside world.

"Have fun, you guys," Theodore's dad said, then quickly turned back to the phone and continued to discuss pay.

Theodore started unpacking the moment his parents left.

"You need help with that?" Nicholas asked.

Theodore turned around and used his index finger to push his massive glasses up the ridge of his nose. "Sure, thanks."

Nicholas struggled to lift the closest suitcase. It must have had forty pounds on him. "What do you have in here?"

"Books."

"Books?" Nicholas unzipped the suitcase and over a dozen Bibles poured out onto the bed. "What do you need all these Bibles for?" He stared. Some were in different languages, Latin, Chinese, Italian…

"I'm studying to be a priest."

*Great. This one's going to be loads of fun.* "Really, that's cool."

"What are you studying to be?" Theodore turned around to face Nicholas, eyes drifting over his shoulder to the posters of bands and athletic stars covering the walls. He raised an eyebrow as his gaze stopped at Dexter's feet sticking out from beneath a pillow. Nicholas quickly adjusted the pillow so that his stuffed bear was completely covered. He was much too old to own a stuffed animal, but he still needed Dexter nearby. It was the only bit of home he had left.

He shrugged. "I'm only sixteen, I've got plenty of time to worry about being an adult later." Honestly, he never thought much of having a future. He could never picture himself old— or even any older than he was now.

Theodore pursed his lips. "I just turned sixteen two weeks ago and I've been planning on being a priest forever."

"Really?"

"Yup, I've been an altar boy for the last seven years. My dad has known Father Henry since he was an altar boy himself. We come from a long line of altar boys."

"Fascinating," Nicholas said. He was becoming an accomplished sarcastic liar. "Well you settle in and I'll catch up with you later. Have fun." He grabbed his jacket and hurried out of the room before Theodore could ask Nicholas to show him around the campus.

Nicholas crossed the dormitory, passing the crowds of students having reunions with friends they hadn't seen all summer. Some of his acquaintances waved as he passed by.

"Hi, Nicholas," the Fenton twins, Kate and Karolyn called

as Nicholas hurried down the stairs to the first floor.

"Nice to see you, ladies." He winked. His confident manner contributed to his popularity among the girls of St. Christopher's Academy. Nicholas made sure his hair was combed neatly and parted to the side to give himself a classic look. His skin was flawless, and being the captain of the sophomore swim team kept him in top shape.

"Hey Nick, what's going on?"

Nicholas gave a high-five to Dean Jackman, co-captain of the swim team. "Nothing much. We all still going to Piccadilly Circus Monday night?"

Dean nodded.

"Awesome. What time are we sneaking out?" Nicholas asked.

"As soon as the sun goes down." Dean laughed. "I think I'm going to invite Becky. You think she'll come?"

"Probably. I heard she's roommates with Jessica this year and I know Jessica is going."

"Good thing I brought the new cologne." Dean smelled the collar of his shirt. "Like a moth to a flame." He cracked his knuckles and flexed his impressive arms. Nicholas smiled. Dean's cockiness made it hard for him to find a date. Besides, Dean wasn't as good-looking as Nicholas. He tried to make up for his simple traits by spending extra time at the gym, but being best friends with Nicholas meant staying in the shadows.

"Did you meet your new roommate?" Dean asked.

Nicholas rolled his eyes. "His name is *Theodore*. He has like *twenty-four* Bibles. Some in different languages and he's studying to be... brace yourself for this... a *priest!*"

Dean laughed in disbelief, but the look on Nicholas's face confirmed he spoke the truth. "No way. He'll be such a nark. How are you going to sneak out Monday night with him as a roommate?"

"I have no idea," Nicholas said as they walked down the hall toward the cafeteria. Hand-made student posters decorated the walls, followed by lockers, then a large painting of the school mascots, a lion and a unicorn in a brawl, portrayed in the school's colors of blue and silver. Doors leading to classrooms lined the walls on either side, with occasional openings to other hallways and corridors.

They entered the cafeteria and chose the only empty table. The room was filled with lounging students and parents who had just helped their kids settle into the dorms. Nicholas always found it hard to watch parents and their kids together. He tried to ignore the activity, reaching for an apple in a basket at the center of the table. "I don't know. Maybe I'll just invite Theodore along. Then he can't rat me out." He took a large bite of the apple, trying to distance himself from the sounds of laughter that overpowered the cafeteria.

"You think he's the type of kid to sneak out of school after hours?" Dean asked.

"No way, but I'm clever. I'll think of something," Nicholas grinned. "Remember you were just a bookworm too, before I corrupted you." He winked.

Just then, he noticed a movement at the entrance of the cafeteria and turned, momentarily forgetting all the activity around him.

The girl that just stepped through the doorway was new— and yet he could swear he had seen her before. Another movie star? It did not seem likely.

She had dark red hair that fell down her shoulders in large curls and the pale complexion of someone whose skin had never been touched by sunlight. But it was her eyes that held him, evoking a forgotten memory, as though Nicholas recognized her as a childhood friend or a character from a past dream. Such an incredible green, as beautiful as a forest with just as many secrets.

Nicholas continued to stare as the girl crossed the cafeteria and made her way to the salad bar. She caught Nicholas staring, pulled back her hair and smiled. A warmth washed through Nicholas, making him strangely eager for more. The cafeteria was obnoxiously loud, buzzing with students, but at this moment, no one mattered but the two of them.

"Who is that?" Nicholas asked.

"Who?" Dean followed Nicholas's gaze. "She's cute. Who knows, probably grade nine."

"No way. She's gotta be our year."

The girl filled her plate with salad, and picked at it while she waited in line to pay. She seemed to be in bliss as she continued eating, as if she had never tried anything so tasty. She stepped out of the line to grab two breadsticks from a nearby bowl and place them on her plate.

"You think she'll come out with us on Monday night?" Nicholas asked.

"How should I know?" Dean said. "Go ask her. I'm going to go get some lasagna. She's making me hungry." He licked his lips and jumped into the line.

Nicholas rose to his feet. He straightened his shoulders and breathed against his hand, sniffing it to make sure it was okay. He put on his most confident look the one that always worked so well with girls, as he walked across the cafeteria. As he approached the new girl, he plucked a flower from a centerpiece on a nearby table, then leaned toward her and waved the flower across her face.

She smiled, but not the way Nicholas had hoped—more awkward than flattered. A look Nicholas was not used to.

"For you." He handed her the flower, flashing her his best smile.

"Thanks." She hesitated a moment, then took the flower and placed it on her tray.

"The name's Nicholas Blackwell." He glanced down to her plate. "That's a lot of salad."

"We don't normally have food like this at home." She picked up her tray and walked away, quickly changing directions as she searched for a seat through the crowded cafeteria. Nicholas followed.

"You don't have salad where you come from?" Nicholas was surprised.

"Not exactly." She placed her tray on the table and took a seat in a booth. Without an invitation, Nicholas scooted in next to her.

"I thought salad was everywhere… What's your name?" He held out for an answer, but she just smiled back. "Come on. I told you mine, now tell me yours. That's kind of how this works."

"This isn't the first time you've been doing this, is it?" she asked.

"Doing what?"

"Picking up a new girl. Giving her a flower you stole from a centerpiece, all in order to draw her in so that you could get a 'phone number'."

"I would never." His voice got higher.

"Sure." She laughed and started to eat her salad.

"So, what is your number? Just joking," he added quickly. "But come on, give me a name. Please…" He smiled, hoping his dimples showed. His smile was usually enough to get what he wanted.

She measured him with a glance, as if deciding if he was worthy. "Amy."

"See, that wasn't so difficult. Amy. Pretty name… So you're new here? I'm guessing you're in grade ten?"

She only nodded.

Nicholas frowned. He was used to new girls being more responsive to his charms. And more forthcoming with information about themselves. They had known each other for ten minutes already and the only thing she'd told him was her name.

"I know how hard it can be to be the new kid," he went on, "so how about this. Some kids in our year are going out to Piccadilly Circus on Monday night. Would you do me the honor of accompanying me?"

She raised her eyebrows. "Off the school grounds?"

Nicholas nodded.

"Isn't that forbidden?"

"That's what makes it exciting," he said.

"Are you still going to go if I don't?"

"It's kind of a tradition. A bunch of us go every year," he admitted. "But it would be so much better if you came."

"Well then, I guess someone's got to keep you out of trouble."

"Awesome!" Nicholas jumped out from the booth. "So it's a date."

"I never said that."

"We'll see," he winked. "Come to room D-104 at sundown on the first day of school. In two days."

# ANOTHER DAY, ANOTHER PUNISHMENT

Nicholas suppressed a shiver as he stepped through the doorway into the most dreaded room in the academy: the principal's office. He avoided making eye contact with Father Henry sitting at an impossibly large desk in front of him. He looked past the priest at the massive window, its heavy drapes pulled back to reveal the school's courtyard. His eyes lingered on the doorway to a small library adjoining the office, then on a stone fountain built into the opposite wall of the office. The statues flanking the fountain were striking: a snarling lion and a burly unicorn, both rearing toward an ornate crown in between. The trickling sound of water in the fountain was soothing, yet it could not bring comfort for what was coming.

He tried to look nonchalant as he settled into the chair across the desk.

"Nicholas," Father Henry said. "Why is it that I find myself staring at you, in my office, the day before the beginning of the new school year?" The priest's hands folded on top of the desk as he leaned forward in his leather chair and glared at Nicholas seated across from him.

Nicholas sighed. "I swear, I have no idea what you're talking about. Honestly. No clue. I didn't do anything wrong."

Father Henry's hands rubbed his forehead in irritation. "So it wasn't you who put thirty-one bottles of shampoo into the school's swimming pool? And it wasn't you who had a private party last night in the woods, with a group of other students?"

Nicholas stared. "Of course not! I am the captain of the swim team. I *swim* in that pool. If the pool is filled with soap, we can't swim. And I would never have a party in the woods." His voice drifted into a higher pitch, then into silence. Perhaps he shouldn't have said this last bit. Why did he always have to be the one to blame for all the parties on campus? Everyone had fun, didn't they?

Father Henry pulled out a drawer at the bottom of his desk. His fingers skimmed through manila folders until he found the one he was searching for. He pulled it out and tossed it on the desk. Written along the edge was Nicholas's name. "This is only last year's claims against you."

"Claims?" Nicholas shifted in his seat. He could already feel his back starting to sweat.

"Yes, claims: assaults, vandalisms, rallies, ditching, destructions, food fights, leaving school grounds, holding parties in your room, countless detentions, numerous offenses. I swear boy, you've given me more trouble in the years you have attended this academy than all the other troublesome boys combined."

"A lot of those other students also got in trouble," Nicholas reminded. "Why aren't *they* under investigation?" He folded his arms across his chest.

"Because you are the leader. You are the conductor of all the mischief in this school."

The name "Conductor Nicholas" in flashing neon lights flickered in his head. It had a nice ring to it.

"Nicholas, I fear your constant ploy against authority will lead you into a barred cage. I understand that the loss of your home and parents has taken its toll, but that was nine years ago.

You are a good student, and you can have a bright future outside this academy—if you allow it. I would hate to see the son of Oliver and Kathleen Blackwell become anything but extraordinary."

Nicholas heaved a breath. His parents had been great students who worked for the school and church for many years. He could never hope to live up to that.

Father Henry lifted his head. "You will assist Gabriel in draining the pool, clean up the mess left in the woods, and help with his chores throughout the week."

"But I didn't do it!" Nicholas jumped out of his chair and paced the blue carpeted office. He had thrown the party in the woods—and perhaps they didn't clean up as well as they should—but there was no way he would ever put soap into the swimming pool. Though, if he confessed to the party, his fate would surely be sealed.

"You will also say four 'Our Fathers' at church this evening," Father Henry's gaze softened. "Nicholas, you're old enough to know right from wrong. Why don't you start doing what's right for a change?"

Nicholas only shook his head as he left the principal's office. He knew Gabriel, the janitor, would be watching him like a hawk now. How was he possibly going to sneak out of the school grounds tomorrow tonight?

As he turned down the hall, pondering clever ways to escape the school undetected, he caught a glimpse of a reptilian tail whipping around the corner.

"What the…" Nicholas hurried after it, turning sharply around the corner, but nothing was there. He let out a sigh. Great. First the trouble in the principal's office, and now his imagination playing tricks on him. Did he party too much last night?

Later that afternoon, after the swim team had met for a preliminary meeting to discuss getting recruits from the new students this year, Nicholas helped Gabriel clean out the swimming pool. He refused to talk to Gabriel for most of the time, much too angry with both the janitor and Father Henry for making him pay for a crime he didn't commit. Although Father Henry did have a point about all the other mischief he caused throughout the years at the academy. But it annoyed Nicholas much more to be punished for something that he didn't do.

After the pool was once again sparkling clean and carried the strong scent of new chlorine rather than shampoo, Gabriel took Nicholas outside the school to the surrounding woods to clean up the trash.

The woods circling St. Christopher's Academy were dense and spread for miles around. Nicholas and Gabriel walked along the damp moss to one of the green meadows hidden within the folds of the sunlight-dappled growth. Thickets filled with the sound of humming insects bordered the meadow. The air was filled with fresh, earthly scents. Nicholas picked some tart-tasting berries as he walked, then grabbed a handful of soda cans and tossed them into his hefty garbage bag.

"Having fun?" Gabriel asked.

Nicholas didn't answer. His garbage bag was becoming almost too heavy to carry. He straightened up to catch his breath, watching Gabriel. The man unnerved him. He always had this smile on his face, even when he was doing the most disgusting job. And he didn't look like a janitor at all. His wavy, light brown hair was well kept, his skin smooth, his features classy. He was also lean, tall, and muscular—even if some of these appealing traits were hard to see in his janitor's jumpsuit.

"Why do you work as a janitor?" he asked. "You're a handsome guy. Young. You seem intelligent. I'm sure you went to school, didn't you?"

Gabriel's grey eyes studied him calmly. "What's wrong with being a janitor?"

Nicholas shrugged. "What isn't?"

Gabriel smiled. "I enjoy being around kids. I take honor in my work. Every job is significant. Each job is just as important as the next."

"I don't think I could ever do this for a living. No matter how much they paid me." Nicholas grabbed a handful of potato chips scattered in the dirt, his face hardened in disgust.

"Are you excited about school tomorrow?" Gabriel asked to change the subject.

"What do you think?" Nicholas smirked and Gabriel couldn't help but laugh. "I had this report to do over the summer, and it's not exactly done."

"It's been three months. What's taking you so long?"

"The report can be on any book we choose, but it needs to focus on how we think God would feel on the book's subject," Nicholas explained. "I swear Sister Agatha has got it in for me."

"Sounds easy enough. It seems like the report is only your personal opinion."

Nicholas looked away. "It's hard to write about God when he has never been there for me."

"You really believe that?"

Nicholas nodded.

Gabriel's eyes narrowed on Nicholas. He hesitated, as if about to say something, then looked away. "I think its time for dinner."

Relieved, Nicholas dropped his garbage bag and took off his stiff rubber gloves. They sat on nearby tree stumps. Gabriel took out two ham sandwiches and passed one to Nicholas.

"I think God watches out for you more closely than you think."

"Doubtful," Nicholas said. "Look what I'm doing. Look where I'm at."

"Perhaps that's the plan."

"Suffering's a plan?" Spending the best years of his life stuck in a boarding school wasn't anyone's idea of a good life.

A quick smile slid through Gabriel's face. "Could be. Suffering strengthens the soul… Do you pray?"

Nicholas shook his head. He was quickly losing interest in the conversation.

"Why not?" Gabriel asked.

Nicholas took a bite of his sandwich, then chewed slowly before responding. "God never answers. I've asked for loads of things. Not just selfish things either. But nothing changes."

"That doesn't mean God isn't listening to you," Gabriel said. "God listens to you all the time. He hears your pleas, and only gives you what he knows you can handle. Sometimes Nicholas, when we pray, the answer is no. Saying no is the hardest thing for God to say, but he does it because he loves you and knows that denying you will strengthen you. One day, Nicholas, you will learn all you were meant to be."

"Cryptic. Didn't think you were so mysterious."

Gabriel smiled again. "There's more to people than what you see. If you want to help around the school, you could always join me. I would like the company and I think it would be good for you. You'll see, Nicholas, that you'll find a great deal of appreciation for God by helping others."

"Thanks Gabriel, but honestly I think believing in God is as pathetic as believing in magic. I think people believe in God because they fear death. People want to know that when they die they don't cease to exist."

Gabriel placed his hand on Nicholas's shoulder. His touch sent a wave of warmth, carrying a strong and overwhelming feeling of comfort beyond anything Nicholas felt before. "Don't fear death, Nicholas, it's only an invitation home."

Nicholas stared. *If God exists, what about me was so undeserving of his love? An invitation home? Where is my invitation? Why did I have to stay behind, while my parents were invited home?*

"Make what you will of death," Gabriel said, "but I assure you, most will experience death not as an enemy, but as a long forgotten friend."

"I'll keep that in mind," Nicholas said. "But it would have to be one hell of an adventure for me to find faith."

Gabriel's hand fell away. "You miss your parents, don't you?"

Nicholas sighed. "How would you feel if you were stuck in this school every day of your life, unable to go home to your family on holidays like most of the other students do? Since I first was brought to St. Christopher's, I have only gone outside those gates a handful of times. I've got nowhere else to go, nowhere I belong. It sucks!"

"I'm sure," Gabriel said, "you are aware that I knew your parents when they attended St. Christopher's Academy and many years after as they worked directly for the Vatican. They were very good people, the best I knew. Loyal, friendly, kind and loving. Great parents. You and your father are so alike. You both share… cunningness. Your dad was a schemer as well."

"Was he really?" Nicholas was intrigued. Normally he didn't care to hear stories about either of his parents, but hearing about his father from Gabriel was unexpected.

"As a student he ran this school." Gabriel winked. "Just know you're not alone. It's often the darkest before the light. You understand, Nicholas?"

"I think so," Nicholas said. He didn't, but it didn't seem a good idea to bring it up.

Gabriel glanced down at his wristwatch. "Church is going to start shortly. You better change into your school uniform." He glanced down at his own clothes. "I better wash up as well."

Together, they gathered up the last of the trash and took

the garbage bags back to school.

Nicholas thought of his parents and how amazing it was that Gabriel had been a janitor when his parents attended the school. He didn't think of it back then, but now as he looked up at the janitor he wondered how that was possible, Gabriel looked no older than thirty. Nicholas hated math, but it was easy to calculate that he should have been barely born when his parents studied here. Did he lie? Or was it a mistake?

A courtyard lay just past the trees and beyond that was the wide, red brick structure of the school. Sometimes Nicholas forgot how truly majestic St. Christopher's Academy was. He rarely saw the building from the outside. But at times like this, when the hazy moonlight in the ink-spilled sky trickled across the red bricks, Nicholas remembered how incredible the school really was.

The building spread low, with four floors of classrooms, dormitories in the West and East Wings, an attic and a basement. An open swimming pool sat in the back next to a courtyard with jungle gyms for the younger students. At the side lay the soccer field, and a quarter of a mile away along a pebble-stone path stood the church, barely visible among the woods. The academy was surrounded on all four sides by the woods as if the school sat in the very eye of the forest.

As a child, Nicholas had pretended St. Christopher's Academy was a medieval castle bordered by an enchanted forest. But those innocent fantasies seemed like a lifetime ago.

Making their way alongside the school, they threw their bags into the dumpsters and parted ways at the entrance. Gabriel continued down the hallway toward his office, while Nicholas ascended the staircase to the boys' dormitory. Students were trickling out from their rooms in their newly washed and ironed school uniforms. Nicholas rushed to his room at the back of the hall, pulling off his shirt as he swung open the door.

As he tossed his dirty shirt on the monitor screen, his eyes settled on Theodore, wrapped in black robes.

"Really?" He stared at his roommate's outfit.

"What's wrong? Did I spill something?" Theodore checked his outfit, searching for a stain. "I knew I shouldn't have eaten spaghetti while dressed for church."

"Why are you wearing robes? You look like Father Henry." Nicholas threw on his white, long-sleeved, collared shirt and began tying a striped tie around his neck.

"I'm helping during mass," Theodore said proudly. "I'll be distributing prayer books."

"Oh, good thing you volunteered. Sometimes the nuns pick students to help and I usually have to duck in my seat."

Theodore rolled his eyes and walked to the door. In the door frame he whipped around to Nicholas and said, "You should be honored to serve the church," before joining the crowds of students heading toward the church.

Nicholas kicked off his pants as he rummaged through his dresser, pulling out a pair of wrinkled black slacks. Dressed, he hurried out of the door and sped down the hall, still tucking in his shirt.

Dean and Nolan waited for him downstairs.

"What's up, guys?" Nicholas asked, falling into stride beside them.

"We recruited Becky Johnson for tomorrow night," Dean said smugly. "I had nothing to worry about. It was a sure thing. I just asked, and she was all for it."

"We heard you got in trouble for last night's party," Nolan said.

"No big deal, just a slap on the wrist." Nicholas curled his lips into a sly smile.

"Was it really you who put soap in the swimming pool?"

"No, someone set me up. But I'll figure it out."

"It's not even the first day of school and you've already been punished." Dean laughed. "That's got to be a St. Christopher's Academy record. Maybe even a world record!"

Nicholas smiled. He hated being punished, but the way Dean and Nolan envied him afterwards made it all worth it. Getting into trouble added to his "coolness."

As they approached the church, Sister Margaret was already shutting the entrance doors. She spotted the three boys leisurely walking toward her and paused to let them through, shaking her head with disapproval.

"Come on now. Quickly."

 # THE SERPENT

Nicholas, Dean and Nolan walked down the polished aisle, wood pews arranged in rows on each side all the way down to the pulpit: a large stage with a podium. A group of chairs up there was occupied by nuns and a handful of altar boys, Theodore included.

Sister Margaret cleared her throat loudly. With lips tightened, she pointed to a bowl of Holy Water. The three boys quickly dipped their fingers into the water and crossed themselves. Sister Margaret ushered them to a nearby pew. As they sat, Nicholas's eyes wandered to the statues lining the walls. Their solemn expressions always made him feel as if he was being watched and judged by each and every one of them.

The choir began singing and most students joined in, reading from their song books. The burning incense and scented candles made Nicholas queasy. He tried to ignore it. He couldn't possibly use his inhaler with Dean and Nolan beside him, not to mention being in the presence of the entire school. He would never show his weakness to anyone.

As the song came to an end, Father Henry walked up to the podium dressed in his most regal robes.

"Welcome, students, to a new year." His voice echoed through the microphone. "First and foremost, I would like to introduce our teachers: Sister Margaret, our Academy's longest lasting nun; Sister Agatha; Sister Nancy; Sister Frances; and Sister Mary. These women will be your instructors during your stay at St. Christopher's Academy. As a reminder, this school was designed by the Vatican as an institution for your education and for your journey through Catholicism."

As Father Henry began to preach, Nicholas's attention drifted away. He was finding the mass tiresome. Constant rising, sitting, bowing, kneeling, praying, always drove him crazy. He fidgeted for a while, but could stand it no longer and darted for the only escape he could think of: the bathroom. He pushed out of the church through the swinging door and made his way to the stand-alone building across the grass.

Nicholas was not overly concerned with hygiene, but he took time to thoroughly wash his hands and use the hand dryer, which kick-started with a loud, annoying screech. Anything beat the boredom of sitting in the church. Once he was finally done, he headed back to the church.

Halfway across the grass, he caught a glimpse of movement. He froze. A large snake rose out of the grass, its triangular head lifting up to Nicholas.

His skin prickled.

Did he just see this thing smile?

"*Thissssss way, Nicholas Blackwell,*" the snake hissed.

Nicholas shook his head, feeling surreal. Was he finally losing his mind? "Did you just speak?"

The serpent glanced at him sideways and lowered back into the grass, heading further into the woods. It looked back a couple of times as if inviting Nicholas to follow. His feet carried him even before he could decide whether this was a good idea.

Like a ribbon in the wind, the serpent led Nicholas deeper and deeper into the forest, until the trees closed around them so densely that he was finding it hard to see the sky. It was quiet down here, too. Nicholas never realized how many sounds he was normally used to in the open air closer to the school.

He pushed through the trees, struggling to keep up with the serpent. Finally, when he felt he couldn't possibly maintain this pace any longer, the serpent stopped at a meadow. A wooden sign stuck out from the ground, leaning slightly to one side. Ivy curled around its base, its leaves reaching up to the words: "Garden of Eden." The serpent slid past it toward an enormous tree with twisting branches and a large curving trunk. Fog rose from the ground here, wrapping its tendrils around the tree. The air smelled of sweet fruits.

The serpent swung its head back to face Nicholas, flicking out its forked tongue. "*Just beyond that tree lies the secret you desire.*" Its long body wormed sideways and wrapped around the wooden sign.

Nicholas stared. Back near the church, he did not have a chance to notice the serpent's eyes—blue and shiny, human. It seemed as if these same eyes looked back at him from the mirror every morning. "*Eat the forbidden fruit. Discover its secrets of good and evil. Become that of God.*"

Entranced, Nicholas advanced. Different feelings coursed through him: peacefulness, curiosity, annoyance, confusion, jealousy, happiness, hatred, anger, guilt…but, most importantly, he felt powerless. His body felt as though it no longer belonged to himself.

"*Go on,*" the serpent persisted.

"Nicholas?"

He spun around toward the strange voice.

Amy stood between the trees, her red hair shining like firelight in the surrounding darkness. The sign that read, "Garden of Eden" had vanished, along with the serpent. Moreover, the enormous tree was gone. Nicholas was standing in an empty meadow surrounded by ordinary maples and oaks.

Nicholas slowly relaxed his shoulders, shaking off the strange vision. He smiled, trying to appear nonchalant. Amy. How in the world did she find him here?

"Did you see that snake?" he asked.

"What snake?" Amy frowned.

He turned around, eyes drifting across the meadow. "It was here a moment ago."

Amy shook her head. "We'd better get back before the nuns find out we're missing."

Nicholas didn't argue. Together they left the meadow and walked back through the woods. Bewildered, Nicholas pondered the whole situation. He knew that the serpent had been there. He saw it with his very own eyes; he heard it speak. *Was that the same one he saw outside Father Henry's office?* His gaze lifted to Amy. *What was she doing in the middle of the forest this late at night?*

"Were you following me?" Nicholas asked, pushing past a thorn bush and whacking vines out of his path.

"No. Well, yes. Sort of. Don't get the wrong idea, but I saw you leave the church, and I went out to follow you. I wanted to talk to you alone. But before I could say anything to you, I saw you head into the woods, so I decided to follow you. I tried to keep up, but you started running." She paused. "I should be asking what *you* were doing running through the woods."

"I thought I saw something."

"The snake?" She seemed amused.

"Yes, the *snake.*"

She shrugged. "I'm sure there are loads of snakes in these woods."

"Not like this one." He glanced around. The woods were silent now.

They entered the field beside the church just as the choir started the last song.

"What did you want to ask me anyway?" Nicholas ran his fingers through his hair.

She lowered her eyes. "I wanted to tell you that I will not be going with you and your friends tomorrow evening."

"Why not?!" He gasped, halting in the middle of the field.

"Let's just say you're not who I thought you were." She hesitated. "Actually you're exactly who I thought you were."

"What the heck is that supposed to mean?" He frowned. Why was he putting so much effort into the conversation?

She sighed. "You're cocky and manipulative and you are used to getting whatever you want."

He raised his eyebrows. "I'm used to getting whatever I want? I live in this school all year round. Even if I wanted to leave, I have nowhere in the world I could possibly go." He stopped himself. How could she, a new girl, possibly understand?

Amy blinked, watching him. "Don't you always get any girl you want?"

Nicholas hesitated. He had had a few girlfriends in the past, and enough experience to realize that any question about previous relationships was usually a trick question. "No."

Amy's lips twitched. "How about Penny Perks, Victoria Michaels, Monica Mitson, Samantha Daniels, Alex Baldridge…"

"Whoa, whoa, whoa." Nicholas held out his hands. "How do you know? What the heck are you? A psychic?"

"Let's just say that the girls' dormitory is filled with conversations about the infamous Nicholas Blackwell."

Nicholas couldn't help a proud smile. *The infamous Nicholas Blackwell.* He liked the sound of it.

He stopped himself as he saw the way Amy rolled her eyes and tossed her red curls over her shoulder.

"That's so not fair," he said. "A couple of bad decisions leave my name in ruins?"

She laughed. "A couple? Aim a little higher."

"Okay, okay. I get it. I'm punished for it. But... I really like you."

"You don't even know me."

"True, but I would like to get to know you. Can't we be friends? Please come with me tomorrow night. I really want you to."

She appeared to hesitate. Nicholas tried to put uncertainty into his eyes; at least the admiration he felt for her wasn't pretended. He smiled hesitantly, knowing that this half-smile would do best to show off his dimples.

"Oh, alright," Amy said.

"Yes!" Nicholas jumped up.

"But only as friends."

"Yeah, of course. Wouldn't try anything. Friends. Buddies. Pals. One of the guys." He stopped, face flushed. "Not one of the *guys*. I meant... just..."

She rolled her eyes. "Just go into the church."

"What about you?" He narrowed his eyes at her.

"I still have to use the restroom."

"Oh yeah. See ya."

Nicholas left her alone and headed into church. He paused in the doorway, watching Amy take several steps toward the bathroom building and hesitate, as if waiting for something. Moments later, Gabriel came out of the restroom with a bag of garbage in his hands. He smiled at Amy like he would to an old friend. From here Nicholas could not see her face, but it seemed to him that Gabriel also gave her the thumbs up before disappearing into the woods.

Nicholas was still thinking about his encounter with the serpent as he entered the church, joining Dean and Nolan in line for communion..

"Did you get stuck?" Dean whispered. Nolan laughed quietly, then went on to repeat the joke several times.

"No," Nicholas said. "A girl."

"Trouble in paradise?" Nolan winked and nudged Nicholas in the ribs.

"Was that the new girl?" Dean asked.

Nicholas nodded.

Dean sighed wistfully. "How do you get into these situations? I just don't understand."

The line moved them closer to Father Henry distributing bread. Nolan received his piece, then Dean. Nicholas stepped up and cupped his hands to hold the little round wafer.

Father Henry nodded to Nicholas. "I trust you said your prayers for forgiveness for your vandalism?"

"Of course." Nicholas smiled broadly. Theodore passed him the goblet of wine, giving him a suspicious glance.

"Where were you? I didn't see you during the entire mass," Theodore asked quietly.

"I have no idea what you're talking about." Nicholas took a sip of wine, wishing he could have more.

After the mass was over, students poured out of the church and headed back to their dorms. Nicholas and his friends steered to the side and headed into the cafeteria for a late night snack. Nolan was a master at picking locks, affording them access after hours.

Before they knew it, it was well past curfew. Nicholas said good night to his friends and wandered slowly back to his room.

Slipping through the hallway, Nicholas held his breath and took cover as two nuns patrolling the school grounds walked past. Sister Agatha, the six-foot tall nun whose long neck and tight cheek bones made her look more like a peacock than a human, did her nightly roam through the dormitories alongside the short and tubby Sister Nancy. They were a nasty pair.

Nicholas quickly snuck past them as they turned up the staircase. He hurried across the lower level of the dormitory and raced up the back staircase. Just as Sister Agatha and Sister Nancy reached the top of the staircase, Nicholas peeked out from his bedroom door.

"You know the exercise video I ordered has done wonders," an out-of-breath Sister Nancy exclaimed. Nicholas stifled a laugh. Sister Agatha stayed silent, and Nicholas imagined her cold sneer as he closed the door. Lucky they weren't the fastest.

He wiped the sweat off his forehead and collapsed onto the bed. He grabbed a tennis ball and bounced it off the ceiling a couple of times, then paused as he belatedly remembered he didn't have the room to himself anymore. He looked around and sighed. Sure enough, Theodore was kneeling at the edge of his bed, hands folded on top of his mattress, eyes closed. He wasn't speaking, but his lips were moving.

"Hey Theo, what're you doing?" Nicholas asked.

Theodore looked at Nicholas with a frown. "Praying." He turned away.

"Whatcha praying about?"

Theodore sighed, then stood up and crawled into bed. "Lots of stuff."

"Like…?"

"Did you hear about that car accident that put that seventeen-year old girl in a coma?"

Nicholas shook his head.

"She was driving home from school, late at night after a choir concert, when a drunk driver ran a red light and smashed into her car. It was all over the news."

"Wow, that's horrible," Nicholas said.

"That's what I was praying about. I asked for her to get better and for her family to keep strong," Theodore said.

"You think praying really helps?"

Theodore nodded. "I pray every day. I believe it helps."

"I haven't prayed since I was seven years old." Nicholas wasn't sure what got him to open up, but words just kept flowing out of him under Theodore's intent gaze. "After my parents died I prayed every night to see them again, but it didn't work. I haven't even seen a picture of them in nine years. I hardly remember what they looked like."

"That's awful," Theodore said. "Do you mind if I ask how they died?"

"Murdered." Nicholas's chest tightened as he remembered looking down the banister at his parents. His breathing turned harsh and he quickly took his inhaler to his mouth and pressed down—quickly, so that Theodore wouldn't notice. Nobody except the nuns and Father Henry knew he had asthma. He didn't want to be known as a weakling—he had a reputation to uphold.

"What were they after?" Theodore asked.

"Me." Nicholas breathed in deeply as his lungs opened up. "I don't know why. All I remember was two men asking my parents what happened to the sins."

"*Sins?* Like the seven deadly sins?"

"What?"

Theodore lifted his head off his pillow and looked at Nicholas in disbelief. "You haven't heard of the seven deadly sins? In a Catholic school?"

"Of course I've heard of them," Nicholas said. "Lust, Gluttony, Greed, Sloth, Wrath, Envy and Pride. So what?"

"Nothing." Theodore shook his head. "It's just when you mentioned the sins I thought…" His voice drifted into silence.

They both were quiet for awhile. Nicholas thought of the seven deadly sins and wondered which had been the one he committed most.

"Hey Nicholas," Theodore said sleepily. "I'll pray for your parents."

The sting in Nicholas's throat kept him from responding. He pulled Dexter out from underneath his pillow and sat the stuffed bear beside him. As he drifted off to sleep, he dreamed of a pair of slit eyes beneath his bed, outlined in the swirling darkness—eyes as blue as the deepest trench of the ocean.

*The serpent hissed.*

# THE ORIGINAL SIN

The next morning, when Nicholas returned from the shower down the hall, Theodore was already gone. He probably left early to find his classes, which wasn't easy for a new student. Nicholas felt bad that he hadn't offered to show him around, but quickly dismissed the thought as he combed his hair and put on his school uniform.

The dormitory halls were empty. Most students were already in class, but Nicholas liked to be fashionably late. At his own pace, he finally made it to Literary Arts where Dean had saved him a seat. The teacher, Sister Agatha, lifted her pointy nose out of a book and waved her finger at Nicholas as he sneaked across the room.

The class was boring, with Sister Agatha droning on about the material they would be learning in the new year. Nicholas did his best to pay as little attention as possible, absorbed in a conversation with Dean about going to Piccadilly Circus that evening. Once or twice he caught Sister Agatha's disapproving gaze, forcing an interruption to the conversation. Nicholas was glad for the school bell that rang to announce the end of the class.

Next, it was off to Algebra, the most dreadful subject in the world, followed by Biblical Studies with his favorite nun, Sister Margaret. She had a soft spot for Nicholas and she often looked the other way when he got out of line. Biblical Studies wasn't Nicholas's favorite class, and he was just settling in for a quiet nap in his seat when the door opened and Amy Glen walked in. Nicholas's heart raced as he instantly sprang to alertness, watching her walk down the aisle.

He thought fast. All the seats around him were occupied. He had to remedy that if he hoped for Amy to sit beside him. Watching her approach out of the corner of his eye, he leaned over and poked the shaggy kid beside him.

"Hey, Nolan. You mind moving across the room?"

"What for?" Nolan sounded insulted.

"A girl," Nicholas mouthed.

Nolan rolled his eyes, grabbed his textbook and shoved it back into his backpack. "You owe me," he said as he headed off to the other end of the classroom.

Nicholas shot up, waving a hand to Amy. "Amy, over here. I saved you a seat."

She smiled and walked toward him, taking a seat at Nolan's old desk. "Thank you."

"Nicholas!" Theodore was walking his way, balancing a stack of books. "Who knew we were in the same class!" He rested his books on a desk, catching his breath.

"Weird," Nicholas agreed.

"Too bad all the seats are taken or we could have sat next to each other," Theodore said.

"You can have my seat." Amy rose to her feet.

"Oh no, I couldn't," Theodore said.

Nicholas grabbed Amy's arm and pulled her down. "He really couldn't," he said through grinding teeth.

"It's no trouble at all," Amy said sweetly, though there was something in that innocent tone that Nicholas recognized as a maneuver he had used before with other girls. Acting nice, while doing his best to avoid someone he was not interested in.

He did this often enough with all those plain girls who craved his attention. He just never imagined it could be done to him. *Am I getting dumped? No, it couldn't be.* Nicholas had never before been turned down by a girl. *Insulting!* He glanced suspiciously from Theodore to Amy as she walked away. They acted smoothly, as if this was all planned. Was he being paranoid?

He rubbed his chin listening to Theodore babbling about getting lost and missing half of his last class. Nicholas didn't pay attention. He was watching Amy as she laughed discreetly in his direction and settled into a chair all the way across the classroom.

Nicholas forced his eyes away and leaned back in his chair, trying to tune out Theodore's constant chatter. How was he going to last a full year sharing a room with Theodore without killing himself? Now Theodore was rambling about the lack of nutritional value in the food at the school's cafeteria. To distract himself, Nicholas opened his notebook and started to take notes as Sister Margaret began her lecture.

"Now, does anyone know the story of the beginning of sin?" Sister Margaret asked.

Sin? Inadvertently, Nicholas remembered last night's conversation. As if on cue, Theodore shot up a hand. The rest of the classroom remained still.

Sister Margaret glanced around. "Really? Only one of you? Come on class, get your minds out of the summer mode. We went over sin in the last few weeks of school before the break." She sighed. "Alright, take it away, Mr. Fink."

Theodore cleared his throat. "The beginning of sin was caused by Eve, the first woman. She ate the fruit from the Tree of Life. The one tree that God commanded not to eat from."

Nicholas's eyes widened. "The Garden of Eden."

All eyes shifted in his direction, before he even realized he had spoken out loud.

"What?" he said to the astonished class.

"That's good, Nicholas." Sister Margaret rose from her desk. "The Garden of Eden is the place where the first sin was committed."

"Is the Tree of Life a big tree?" Nicholas asked, remembering last night's events.

Sister Margaret raised her eyebrows. "I would imagine so. It should look very different from an average tree. Let's not forget that the Tree of Life is also known as the Tree of Knowledge of Good and Evil. God permitted Adam and Eve to eat the fruit from any of the trees in the garden, but not from the tree that gives knowledge of good and evil."

Theodore nodded. "The serpent tempted Eve to eat the forbidden fruit. Eve committed the first sin."

"But didn't the snake commit a sin first?" Nicholas asked.

The students and Sister Margaret continued to stare at Nicholas. He was surprised at himself. Never before did he feel compelled to show such interest in a school subject.

"What kind of sin did the snake commit?" Sister Margaret asked.

"Greed?"

She shook her head. "Greed would have been if the snake kept the forbidden fruit for himself."

"Then Pride?"

Sister Margaret looked at him with interest. "Why Pride?"

"Because the snake took pride in his cleverness. The snake clearly knew that Adam and Eve were not to eat the forbidden fruit. He was probably bored, so he tricked Eve into eating the fruit and giving it to Adam."

"Excellent theory," Sister Margaret said. "Why am I not surprised, Nicholas, that the one time you take part in a lecture is when the topic relates to sin?" These words were answered by a few chuckles from across the room. But Nicholas also saw interest on the faces of the students as the discussion continued.

"The snake is an animal, how could an animal sin?" Nolan asked from his seat.

"The Bible says that the snake was the most clever of all God's animals," Sister Margaret said.

"I thought the snake was the Devil," Theodore pointed out. "That's how mom always told me the story." This provoked a few giggles from around the room. Sister Margaret silenced them with a glance.

"Some believe the snake was Lucifer disguised," the nun said. "Others believe the fallen angel sent the snake to do his bidding. Either way, the snake and all its ancestors have been forever punished for the sin. It is written that the snake would forever walk on his stomach and in all his days he would eat dust. His legs would be removed as payment for his crime."

"But wouldn't sin have been born way before the snake tricked Eve?" Nicholas asked.

Sister Margaret paused, once again eyeing him with interest. "How so?"

"Well, even if Lucifer wasn't the snake, he obviously was a fallen angel by then, or he wouldn't have sent the snake. Right? So if Lucifer was a fallen angel already, clearly he had sinned somehow."

"Perhaps." Sister Margaret nodded. "So that alone could be a debate. When did Lucifer fall from grace?"

"Right before the war," Amy answered. Eyes throughout the classroom now shifted in her direction.

"What war, Miss Glen?"

"Between the angels." Amy spoke slowly, as though remembering a dream. "Angels fought in a battle for Heaven. The archangels forced the fallen angels out of Heaven with the Sword of Michael. The Sword was said to be the only thing that could harm Lucifer, because the blade was forged from Lucifer's blood and the tears he brought to God's eyes for betraying him."

"I've never heard this version," Sister Margaret said.

All eyes turned to Amy.

Sister Margaret moved between the aisles as she spoke. "Many different interpretations of the Bible stories have been told throughout the centuries. Stories have been handed down from each generation for thousands of years. So of course some differ from family to family." Sister Margaret smiled. "But I do think that's fascinating, Miss Glen, about the Sword of Michael. It has somewhat of a fantasy ring to it, doesn't it?"

At that moment the school bell rang, ending the lesson. All the students instantly sprang to life, picking up backpacks, shoving books and folders under their arms.

Sister Margaret raised her voice to be heard above the chatter. "Alright, tonight's homework is to write a one page essay on the beginning of sin. I want to know what you think is the first sin. Have a good day. Enjoy your first day of classes!"

Nicholas caught up with Amy in the crowd of students rushing through the hall. "We still on for tonight?" He asked as he joined her on the walk to her next class.

She nodded, "Your room at sundown, right?"

"Yup, you're going to have a blast. Piccadilly Circus is so much fun. It's just a few miles away, in London. There are a lot of cool shops, a big theatre, people put up tents and sell things they make. It's really fun."

"I'm excited," Amy said, though she didn't seem too enthused about sneaking out. Then she glanced past Nicholas and called out, "Theodore!"

Nicholas spun around and saw Theodore, who stood nearby searching a map for his next classroom. The boy looked up, finger pushing his glasses up his nose.

"Are you going to come with us tonight?" Amy asked softly.

Nicholas covered his face with his hand. *This is not happening!*

"Where are you guys going?" Theodore asked.

"A bunch of us are going to Piccadilly Circus tonight," Nicholas said gloomily.

"Piccadilly Circus!" Theodore exclaimed.

Nicholas hushed him as a group of nuns walked past them. When they were out of sight, Theodore leaned closer to Nicholas and Amy. "Piccadilly Circus is off school property and is absolutely *forbidden* without authorization from Father Henry himself."

Nicholas rolled his eyes. "If you do this for me, I'll do something for you in return."

"Something?"

"Anything you ask me to."

"Okay," Theodore said faster than Nicholas had anticipated.

"Really?" Nicholas had a sinking feeling he had just made a very bad bargain. Theodore was weird. Who knew what he would ask of Nicholas.

"I'll do this for you," Theodore said solemnly, "if you agree to pray."

"Pray?" Nicholas frowned in surprise. Out of all the things Theodore could have asked from him, praying was the last thing that came to mind. He could have asked Nicholas to make him popular, get him on the swim team, do his homework (though Nicholas wouldn't be able to give him the best grade). He could have asked for *anything* and he chose praying?

"Deal." Nicholas said.

They confirmed it with a handshake.

"What's your next class?" Nicholas asked.

Theodore looked forlorn. "Gym."

Nicholas nodded. "I have a swim meet next period. It's right by your gym class. Might as well take you there." He turned to Amy. "Remember, my room at sundown. Got it?" He winked.

"Got it."

Nicholas led Theodore out of the building to the field beside the pool, where kids in Theodore's next class were lined up and starting to stretch.

Theodore took a deep breath. "Farewell Nicholas, I thank you with utmost gratitude." He waved uncertainly and hurried to his class.

*Does he really have to talk like that? Is he purposely trying to sound like a nerd?* To look like a short and tubby junior priest in oversized glasses was one thing; looks were hard to change. But why did he have to talk weird too?

Nicholas's lips lifted into a cocky smile as he directed his thoughts to tonight. Everything was coming together for the trip to Piccadilly Circus. He had a date with the most gorgeous girl in school, Theodore promised not to rat him out, even if this came at the price of bringing the boy along. Everything was perfect, Nicholas thought as he headed to a swim meet.

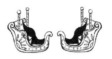

# PICCADILLY CIRCUS

Sundown came fast. Nicholas and Theodore's room quickly filled up as Amy, Nolan, Dean, Jessica and Becky arrived all at once. They kept quiet, waiting for Sister Agatha and Sister Nancy to pass through the hallway outside the bedroom door. Nicholas stood guard with his ear pressed to the door, his friends talking in half-whisper. He couldn't help smiling as he watched Dean's attempts to flirt with Becky using Nicholas's own clever pickup lines. He turned his attention to Amy and Theodore at the desk. Theodore was flipping though one of his Bibles showing Amy his favorite verses. Amy listened attentively. Nicholas's eyes paused on the curls of her auburn hair tucked behind her ears, then moved over to Nolan, lying on his bed, bouncing a baseball off the ceiling. Jessica sat beside him, chewing gum with a bored look on her face.

"Why are we hiding in here?" Jessica asked. "Students don't have to be in their rooms for another three hours."

"Because once they pass our hallway, Sister Agatha and Sister Nancy will go to the girls' dormitory leaving the side entrance free," Nicholas said for the fourth time since Jessica had arrived.

She twirled a strand of her hair, dyed to a perfect platinum blonde. "Whatever."

Nicholas rolled his eyes. Jessica took out the magazine she brought and started skimming through the pages, searching for the latest gossip.

"Hey, that's Mom." Theodore pointed to the magazine.

Jessica lifted her eyes from the article, her long eyelashes fluttering. She looked him up and down, as if just noticing he was in the room. "This," she pointed violently to the picture beside the article she was reading, "is the one and only Julia Fink. Retired *model*, brilliant *actress*, leading star in *The Last Crime of Charles Dotson*, soon to premier in a new series with my soon-to-be husband, Christopher Hayes."

All eyes in the room fell on Jessica. Theodore looked almost too scared to speak. With a gulp, he stuttered, "Sh…sh… sh… she's my… my… my… mom."

"You wish." She turned away and buried herself back into her magazine.

For a moment, Nicholas was about to tell Jessica that Julia Fink was really Theodore's mom, but then he thought that Jessica just might have a fit, or worse, kill him for not introducing them. He turned back to the door, listening. "Alright we've got to go, now."

They walked quietly through the hall and hurried down the stairs. Nicholas skipped two steps at a time until he reached the side entrance. He opened the door and peeked outside. His heart raced as he saw Father Henry come out from the school and climb into the limo waiting outside. *Where does Father Henry go when he leaves St. Christopher's Academy?* For a moment, Nicholas imagined the priest playing miniature golf, holding on to a mustard-smeared hot dog and slurping an icee. He shook his head. Father Henry wasn't the fun type, he always looked like he was headed to a secret government mission. As the limo drove off, Nicholas couldn't help but wonder what his priest was up to now.

When the coast was clear they followed the road toward the gate, staying close to the edge of the woods in case they needed to hide from passing cars. Nicholas led the way. Amy came behind him, next to Theodore who looked very nervous, eyes darting around in panic. As they walked, Nicholas could hear Amy's soothing voice. He was glad she was able to calm Theodore down. It was her fault they had to bring him along. He glanced further down the line, noticing Dean make another failed attempt to hold Becky's hand and Nolan pick up some pebbles and start juggling them as he walked—no doubt to distract himself from Jessica's constant complaints.

The iron gate at the school entrance stood wide open, flanked by the gargoyle statues that always gave Nicholas the creeps. The taxi van Nicholas had called for waited for them on the side of the road. They all got in.

"Piccadilly Circus, please," Nicholas said and the taxi was off.

By the time they got to Piccadilly Circus it was getting dark. Crowds of people flooded the streets and filled the shops. Bright store signs shone overhead. Jessica stopped at every glass window displaying the newest fashions, beaming with excitement.

Dozens of open stalls lined the sidewalk, displaying all sorts of handmade goods—an assault of colors and shapes that made Nicholas feel dizzy. He looked further ahead toward the broad theater building that towered over the rest. Posters of the latest box office hits lined the walls. The air rang with sounds—laughter, soft music playing on the speakers hidden in bushes and trees, people talking on cell phones. Life at its brightest, so different from the dreary reality of St. Christopher's Academy.

Nicholas took a full breath of the evening air, a smile tugging at the corners of his mouth. He was always waiting for these trips—the first and last day of school when he could come to London. The only times when he didn't feel trapped.

Their group stopped abruptly as Jessica grabbed Becky's hand and tugged her toward the closest shop. Halfway there, the girls turned around.

"Amy, you want to come shopping?" Jessica asked.

"No, thanks," Amy said with a smile.

Becky frowned, then glanced at Nicholas wistfully.

"We'll catch up with you guys in a few," Jessica said, pulling her along with a firm hand.

"See you soon, beautiful," Dean smiled and waved to Becky, but the girls were already running for the nearby clothing store.

"Oh sweet, an arcade!" Nolan pointed to the second floor to a store between the theater and the food court. The sounds of electronic games screeched, loud even from where they stood.

"I'm game," Dean said, and the two boys ran off to the arcade, leaving Nicholas, Theodore and Amy standing together on the sidewalk.

Nicholas led them slowly down the crowded street, past all the stands. At the corner they stopped to watch the street entertainers: a man juggling fire-torched clubs, a girl on a unicycle, a magician halfway into a disappearing act, and an elderly man with a large snake wrapped around his shoulders. The snake was yellow, its shiny scales reflecting the colors of the street lights.

As they neared, the snake dropped down to the sidewalk and pointed its face in Nicholas's direction. His skin crept as he hastily looked away. He hadn't minded snakes before, but lately they had started to become unnerving.

He led the way into a book shop. He hoped books would make a good distraction for Theodore, keeping his roommate occupied so that he and Amy could finally get some time alone. He was right. Theodore's eyes lit up as he hurried into the religion section, disappearing between the shelves.

Nicholas and Amy sat on a couch in the middle of the shop. A coffee machine nearby spread a pleasant aroma.

"You look really pretty tonight." Nicholas put on his charm. He reached past her and grabbed a handful of chocolates from a small glass bowl and shoved them into his pocket to snack on later.

"Thank you." Her eyes followed him, her frown betraying irritation.

Nicholas felt taken aback. "What? There's a sign saying the chocolates are complimentary."

Amy rolled her eyes, then glanced away.

Nicholas felt nervous. Courting new girls had surely been easier before. Amy was a tough nut to crack.

"Are you having fun?" he asked.

She nodded. "I can't believe this place is only a few miles from our school. It seems like a different world. I can see why you wanted to come."

"We come here twice a year, on the first and the last school day," Nicholas said. "We haven't gotten caught yet," he added proudly.

Amy nodded again, her gaze trailing away as if she was losing interest.

*Focus on her. Ask her something, so she can talk.* "So how did you end up coming to St. Christopher's?"

She smiled distantly. "It's a long story."

"We have time."

"Not enough." She looked away again, her eyes following the bright turmoil outside.

Nicholas sighed. Clearly Amy didn't care to talk about herself. Perhaps a more physical approach would work?

He inched closer and casually sneaked an arm around her shoulders. Amy stiffened, but before she could respond, they heard a loud crash from between the shelves where Theodore had disappeared to earlier. Nicholas swore inwardly as they both jumped up and ran to the noise.

Theodore was kneeling among a pile of books that had apparently fallen from the shelf, picking them up. Amy suppressed a smile and rushed to help him. Nicholas only shook his head. Every time he got close to Amy, Theodore had done something to shatter the moment. Was this all a coincidence? Or was his roommate doing this on purpose?

Suddenly Nicholas could not bear the sight of Amy and Theodore side by side.

"I'm going to go check on Dean and Nolan," he said and headed out of the shop.

He walked down the street, passing the juggler and the old man, whose snake was no longer around, and continued through the outdoor mall. Halfway to the arcade, a movement caught his eye. He stopped, his skin creeping once again.

The snake was right in front of him, slithering toward a side alley. As Nicholas watched, it shed its skin leaving the long yellow casing crumpling on the floor. It glanced at him briefly, as if inviting him to follow.

Unthinkingly, Nicholas turned into the alley in its wake.

The snake rose up and turned around, facing him. "*Thisssss way.*"

The voice was the same he heard in the woods near the Academy. Entranced, Nicholas watched the snake's scales darken to an arctic blue.

The snake moved again, its glances beckoning him to follow. They went down the alley, past a group of rats. The air became damp as the sounds of the market suddenly fell away. The brick walls on either side of them turned into trees and the paved walkway into a bed of grass. Mist crept low over the ground, partially hiding the serpent from view.

Nicholas kept following, more curious than ever. A lush garden erupted around them. Trees bent their branches low under the weight of fruits. Exotic flowers blossomed everywhere.

An ambush of feelings crawled up his skin. He felt powerless. This would have been such a peaceful garden, if not for the serpent. There was something wicked, maleficent about the creature.

A massive tree rose in the middle of the garden — a tree unlike any other. As Nicholas approached it, entranced, he nearly stumbled over the old sign sticking out of the ground. "The Garden of Eden". His skin prickled. Did the serpent bring him to the same place again? But how?

The serpent slid up the curving trunk of the huge tree onto a nearby branch. Entranced, Nicholas approached.

The branch in front of him held the most beautiful red apple. A drop of moisture glistened on its skin. As he stepped toward the fruit Nicholas felt hungry, starving. He had never felt so hungry in his entire life. He had forgotten what food tasted like, what it felt like for his stomach to be full.

He reached out for the apple.

"*Go on, my child,*" the serpent hissed, "*take a bite.*"

Nicholas froze as he heard cracking sounds, someone tearing through the thick forest's growth. Footsteps rustled on the grass behind him.

"What is this place?" Amy's voice asked.

Nicholas turned around, watching Amy approach him. Her eyes widened, her face contorting in fear as she saw Nicholas reaching for the apple.

"Nicholas, no!"

Too late. Nicholas couldn't stop his hand as he pulled the apple from the stem and bit into it.

How could a fruit taste so good? Sweet and tart, all at the same time. He stood there, chewing, the sweet juice dripping down his chin.

The serpent dropped to the ground and slithered toward Amy. Amy screamed, but before the creature could reach her, it dove into the ground head-first and disappeared.

Nicholas rushed toward her. "What's going on?"

"Do you have any idea what you have just done?"

"Not a clue."

The ground rumbled, making them step closer to each other.

"Your face." Amy pointed.

Nicholas raised his hand to wipe his chin, then held up his hand, and gasped. The juice he wiped off looked red—like blood. He raised it to his nose, the thick smell of blood hitting his nostrils. *Blood?*

Before he could react, the serpent shot up from the ground right in front of them. It grew, its face as big as a minivan, and as it swung toward them, bits of earth showered off its body. Blue eyes glared down upon them.

The serpent then spoke, "*You have eaten the forbidden fruit from the Tree of Life. You have committed the greatest defiance against your Lord Almighty.*"

Nicholas and Amy huddled closer.

"*Nicholas Blackwell,*" the serpent said. "*Seventeen years ago your parents trapped the seven deadly sins in your innocent blood. Only a true act of sin could release them. Because you ate the forbidden fruit you have unleashed the seven Princes of Hell.*"

Nicholas opened and closed his mouth several times, trying to find his voice.

"Act of sin?" he demanded. "All I did was eat an apple!"

The serpent smirked. "*So did Eve, to condemn all humanity.*"

"But…" Nicholas glanced around helplessly. Amy was watching him wide-eyed. The fear in her gaze made his stomach wrench. He had done something terrible.

He turned back to the serpent. "And what will happen now?" He was aware of how his voice came out small, as if smothered by the forest around them.

"*Now, humanity will suffer because of you, as sins once again roam freely in the world.*" The serpent seemed to savor the words, as if enjoying their taste.

"No." Nicholas shook his head. "No."

The serpent paused, its eyes lighting up with a strange gleam. "*No? Whatever do you mean by that, Nicholas Blackwell?*"

"There must be a way for me to undo this."

The serpent froze. Out of the corner of his eye Nicholas saw Amy lift her face in hope.

"I demand a chance to redeem myself!" Nicholas's voice acquired force as he spoke, ringing clearly through the silence. It seemed as if even the leaves stopped their rustling, listening to his words.

The serpent slowly coiled down to the ground, until its face leveled with Nicholas. "*You will risk your life and your soul?*"

"Yes." To his surprise Nicholas realized that he meant it.

"*Very well,*" the serpent said. "*Even though you probably don't know it, boy, you have invoked your ancient birthright. Like a true Blackwell, you have the right to challenge the Princes of Hell. Succeed, and your sin will be undone. Fail, and say farewell to your life.*"

Nicholas nodded, amazed at how he felt no fear or hesitation. "Done."

Amy stepped forward to Nicholas. She stood straight, so different from the scared girl that huddled beside him just moments ago. Nicholas's eyes widened in surprise.

"Great Serpent, let me go with him." Amy's voice rang through the clearing, confident and powerful.

Nicholas stared.

The serpent looked amused as he leaned toward Amy, eyeing her.

"*You would risk your life to save this boy?*"

Amy quickly glanced over to Nicholas and then back to the serpent. "I would."

The serpent lifted an inquisitive eye. *"You are not what you seem, are you, girl?"* It didn't wait for Amy to answer. *"You may accompany Nicholas Blackwell in his fight against sin. But if you do not defeat the Princes, then you as well will be their sacrifice."*

"Deal," Amy said.

"Are you kidding me?" Nicholas couldn't stop staring. Was this the same Amy he knew? And what in the world was going on?

Amy stepped back to his side. "I'll explain everything later."

The serpent hissed. *"A deal has been made. So take a look into the unknown world of Demonio, the very city of demons."* The serpent opened its enormous mouth and it became an archway that revealed a gaping entrance. Its slit tongue bent and twisted into a stairway. Amy took the lead, climbing the stairs.

"You have got to be kidding," Nicholas said, wide-eyed. "This has to be a dream."

"Come on." Amy beckoned him with a wave of her hand.

With no more hesitation, Nicholas stepped onto the staircase.

# ALL THE WAY DOWN

Mucus dripped down the walls of the serpent's mouth as they entered. They traveled through the belly of the serpent until they reached a door.

An elevator door.

A red-tinted salamander stepped out of the shadows. His skin oozed with slime. A tight, button-down vest wrapped around his thin frame. He stood near a rickety old stool in the corner of the elevator, beside the metal door.

"Good day," the salamander said. "Going down?"

"I guess so," Nicholas said, fighting the surreal feeling. He had just spoken to a snake and entered its mouth, to find an elevator inside its belly. There should be nothing wrong with a talking salamander.

He followed Amy into the elevator car.

The salamander pointed to five glowing buttons on the wall near where he stood.

Down

Further Down

Deep Down

Almost Down

All The Way Down

"Which will it be, folks?" inquired the salamander.

"Are those the different floors?" Nicholas wondered.

"Certainly."

Nicholas exchanged a questioning glance with Amy.

"Well, I suppose we should go 'all the way down'," Amy suggested.

Nicholas only shrugged. He didn't relish the thought, but he also knew deep inside that Amy was right. It had to be all the way down, with a slim chance of ever coming back.

"As you wish." The salamander grabbed a handle and turned to Nicholas and Amy. "You two might want to hold on to something."

After a quick jolt, the elevator shot downward with incredible speed. Nicholas imagined his stomach must be miles above, racing to catch up with him. Then, just as suddenly, they crashed to a stop. Lights in the elevator flickered weakly. Sliding doors pulled apart to reveal...

A bookshop.

"Welcome to 'Ramiro's Novels and More'," announced the salamander. Just as Nicholas was about to step out from the elevator, the salamander stopped him. "Don't forget your things." He handed Nicholas his backpack. Nicholas rubbed his chin. He didn't remember bringing it along.

They slowly and cautiously stepped out of the elevator and entered the shop. Its glossy floor was lined with redwood, a maze of tall bookcases running out of sight. Dusty old manuscripts inhabited the shelves along with the brilliant designs of spider webs. The air was infused with magic, a lingering presence that Nicholas instantly recognized, even though he could swear he had never sensed it before.

"What are you doing, coming from that door?" a harsh voice spoke.

They turned around to the back of the shop, where a haggard

old creature sat on a high-up chair beside a hefty cash register. *A demon?* Nicholas had no idea what demons looked like, but he could easily imagine them just like this.

The demon's snout hung with thick wrinkles, his eyes as droopy as those of a blood hound. Sparce strands of white hair corkscrewed off his purple-dotted skull. A white beard fell down his chest and coiled into his lap.

Nicholas glanced back to the elevator, hoping they could jump back on and head to a different floor, but the elevator was no longer there, just a red brick wall.

The creature's gray, wet nose sniffed toward them. "What is that awful scent you bring into my shop?"

"Pugdush believes it to be *good*, Master." A small demon came out of a pair of swinging doors, carrying a stained-glass hookah twice his size. He placed the hookah beside the older creature and handed him an attached hose.

This small demon did not look as ugly as his master—two feet tall, with a face that resembled that of a dog—the sort that a rich woman might carry around in her purse. He was bipedal and had a long tail, like a small monkey. Overall, he looked like a creature straight out of a cartoon.

"Good, did you say?" The old demon took the hose. "That door is not to be used for entry or exit. Neither can be done, nor should it be done. Either way, it is foolish to have been done." His old, leather lips pinched the hose of the hookah. Thick clouds of smoke poured from his mouth and quickly fogged the shop.

"We're sorry." Nicholas swatted the smoke away.

"You're sorry?" The old creature leaned out from his seat. "What sort of demons apologize?"

"Stupid ones." The little demon spat. "Pugdush believes these two strangers to be human."

"Humans? With intact souls?" The demon's droopy eyes lifted in surprise.

"Yes," Amy said.

"Quite interesting. Wouldn't you agree, Pugdush?" The demon looked down to his companion who nodded dully. His gaze returned to Nicholas and Amy. "I am Ramiro, keeper to the entrance of the City of Demons. And this is my apprentice, Pugdush. Who might you two be?"

"I am Amy Glen and this is Nicholas Blackwell," Amy introduced them.

"Blackwell?" Ramiro's eyebrows lifted, crunching his forehead. "Now, I am surely intrigued. The last living Blackwell has come to Demonio at last. Do you share the family legacy?"

"What legacy?" Nicholas asked.

"What legacy? My dear boy, demon seekers." The demon inhaled more smoke from his hose. "Why, I believe your parents were the very best. True seekers. The Champions of Sin."

Pugdush offered them tea. They each took a cup, afraid to show disrespect by declining.

The little demon's face scrunched up with confusion as he examined their clothes. "Interesting garments. You must be very important in your world." He tugged on Nicholas's striped tie.

Nicholas snatched his tie out from the demon's tiny, hairy hands. "They're our school uniforms. Nothing impressive." He shifted back to Ramiro. "I'm sorry, but what do you mean by Champions of Sin?"

"The seven great Guardians of Sin," Ramiro huffed. "You know nothing. Demonio is a city just outside the gates of Hell, where demons dwell. In this city, there are seven rulers who make up the Princes of Hell. Each one is Guardian of a deadly sin. Sixteen years ago, these sins were contained by Oliver and Kathleen Blackwell. Your parents trapped them within an innocent, an unborn child, which of course was you. The Great Serpent sought out the blood of the innocent so that the Princes may reawaken and rule once again."

Nicholas pressed his hand against his head, trying to ease his growing headache. Ramiro continued unsympathetically, "Each of the Guardians has a piece of one Crown. These pieces have morphed from the individual sin, ultimately becoming a different type of object that represents the sin, giving each one unique individuality. Combining these pieces would reconstruct the Devil's Crown and open the Mankind's World to the fury of demons. Since the beginning, demon seekers have sought out the Devil's Crown hoping to keep it hidden from the devil himself in order to assure the safety of the Mankind's World."

Pugdush began to sniff the air. His eyes widened, and a smile spread across his face. He followed the pleasant scent, stopping at Nicholas's pocket.

"Get out of there." Nicholas swatted Pugdush away.

Pugdush pointed a small, leathery finger toward Nicholas's pocket. "You have chocolate? Pugdush smell such deliciousness." He sniffed again. "Two milk chocolates. Four dark chocolates and…" He sniffed again. "One mint chocolate."

Nicholas reached into his pocket and pulled out a handful of the chocolate candies. He examined each piece and was surprised to find Pugdush had guessed each flavor perfectly. "What a nose." He tossed Pugdush a dark chocolate. Without unwrapping it, Pugdush tossed the candy into his mouth.

"Anyway, why doesn't the Devil just take back his Crown himself?" Nicholas felt as if stuck in a dream, no harm in playing along for the moment.

"A treaty was made long ago protecting the pieces of the Crown from anyone but the Guardians. Only one could snatch all the pieces of the Crown and reconnect them as one. A Blackwell would be the one and only protector," Ramiro answered. "Hence, the Blackwell family legacy."

"What does my family have anything to do with the Devil's Crown?" Nicholas asked.

"Much is a secret, even to demons. The only thing understood by demonic souls is that it can only be a Blackwell who could be a true Champion of Sin. Meaning, only a Blackwell may defeat the sins."

Nicholas felt light-headed. What sort of secrets did his parents conceal? How did they connect to sins? The mystery sparked his imagination to unlimited possibilities.

"Why would you help us?" Amy asked. "Wouldn't demons want the Devil to obtain his Crown? It sounds like it would be beneficial to all demonkind."

Ramiro grunted, "Demons, yes, but we Risen demons separate ourselves from the wicked."

"Risen?"

"Pugdush and Ramiro are Risen demons," Pugdush answered, hands raised to hips. "We have stripped our demonic ways, in hope of one day being part of the Divine. Much like the opposite to a fallen angel."

Nicholas frowned. "I don't understand. Am I supposed to fight these Guardians?"

"If you ever hope to leave Demonio, you will challenge the Guardians and obtain their piece of the Devil's Crown. Once you've taken their pieces of the Crown, you may leave Demonio and return to the Mankind's World," Ramiro answered.

"Oh, that's all?" Nicholas couldn't help the sarcasm.

"We have to get you two scented." Pugdush scurried across the glossy floorboards and headed for a nearby table. Lined along the table were three antique perfume bottles, each one a different color: red, blue and purple.

"What will it be," Pugdush pointed to each bottle, "wet dog, clogged toilet or spoiled milk? Pugdush prefers clogged toilet."

"Ew."

The little demon smiled proudly. "Makes Pugdush popular with girl demons."

"I think I'll pass."

"You must pick a scent. Otherwise, the smell of a human is too easily recognized by demons. You wouldn't last long here in Demonio," Ramiro explained.

Nicholas and Amy exchanged worried looks.

Nicholas sighed. "Might as well. Hit me with wet dog."

"Not clogged toilet? Are you sure?"

"Not a chance. Wet dog, please." Nicholas stretched out his arms and circled in place while Pugdush snatched the purple bottle and sprayed. A mist of grey surrounded them.

Amy plugged her nose.

Pugdush sniffed in their direction. He smiled. "Good. Now you reek."

"No kidding." Nicholas's eyes watered.

"On to the challenge at hand," Ramiro remarked from his pedestal. He lifted an old, crooked finger toward Nicholas. "We can help each other. I wish for the Devil's Crown to keep it safe from the demonic. We Risen hope to have it secured in our Chapel of Dreams."

"What's the Chapel of Dreams?" Nicholas asked.

"Never mind that," Ramiro grunted. "If you survive the Guardians and conquer the deadly sins, you will bring me the seven pieces so I may construct the Devil's Crown and keep it safe. I will allow you passage home to the Mankind's World and give assistance along your journey."

"What sort of assistance?" Amy asked.

"The only sort you'll get," Ramiro said flatly. "My sort. Otherwise, face the Guardians alone. Unaided. Unsupported. Ignored. Is that understood?"

"Risen demon or not, you still are a demon nonetheless," Amy pointed out. "The Devil's Crown must be a priceless possession."

"Quite irreplaceable," Ramiro said through clenched teeth.

Nicholas stepped forward. "Why should we put trust in you

and your chapel to secure the safety of such treasure as the Devil's Crown?"

The demon leaned forward. "The Chapel of Dreams is a sanctuary of purity. Understand that Demonio is a city of incredible darkness. I can't stress the obstacles of fear and despair that await you here. Lurking demons terrorize the streets, bringing with them an endless reign of horror. This city is where the creatures of nightmares are born." Ramiro's face softened. "Do not make the mistake of thinking that I am evil. I might appear frightening, but you know not of evil by speaking with me."

Nicholas tried to wrap his mind around Demonio and the seven Guardians that awaited. Excitement and fear rose within him, tightening under his skin. How many times did he dream of an adventure outside the gates of St. Christopher's Academy? Too many to count. The thrill overwhelmed him, lifting a cocky smile on his face. Like his parents had done before him, Nicholas was going to face demons.

"Go on. Go forth," Ramiro twirled the hookah hose between his gnarled fingers. "The longer you wait, the more susceptible you become to the misery of it all. The first sin awaits."

"How do we find the Guardians?" Nicholas asked.

Ramiro sucked the mouthpiece of the hookah, and blew a thick, blinding cloud of smoke that engulfed Nicholas and Amy. The two of them coughed and fanned the smoke away from their faces. By the time the smoke cleared, they were no longer in Ramiro's shop, but in the middle of a dark forest.

 THE MANSION

Bare trees the color of ash surrounded them, their branches reaching down as if ready to grab them at any moment. The ground beneath them looked barren, dried and stone-hard, covered with an infection of tiny fissures.

"What just happened?" Nicholas's head pounded, dizziness settling in as violent as a migraine. His eyes searched through the silent dark wilderness. "Which way should we go?"

Icy wind whistled and brushed across his face, tossing his hair away from his eyes, turning his cheeks blue.

Without saying a word, Amy lifted a finger and pointed. Nicholas followed her finger to a sign that read ONWARD.

"Why not?" Amy said as she started forward toward the sign.

"Why not? I can give you plenty of reasons 'why not'," Nicholas said as he followed Amy through the woods. "This is *so* not a good idea."

"You're the one who asked where to find the Guardians," Amy mocked.

"I thought this was a dream."

"Try a nightmare."

"How is this possible? How is *any* of this possible?" Nicholas said as they continued through the forest. He glared at Amy as he walked beside her. "I've gotten myself into plenty of situations, but this…?"

She shrugged. "Perhaps you shouldn't have eaten the forbidden fruit."

"It was an *apple*, for Pete's sake. How was I supposed to know I couldn't eat it?"

"There's a reason for the word *forbidden*." Amy pursed her lips, trudging ahead.

"What about you?" Nicholas asked, hurrying after her.

"What about me, exactly?"

"Why did you follow me?"

She swallowed, suddenly serious. "Nicholas, I'm not allowed to say."

Nicholas hurried to level up with her. "Well, my guess is you didn't go to St. Christopher's Academy for the academics. What gives? Start talking."

She held a pause. "Let's just say I work for the Vatican."

"Really?" Nicholas stared. "Have you ever seen the Pope?"

She silenced him with a glance. "There are rumors about a city where demons live. The people I work for had me go to St. Christopher's Academy and search for the entrance to this city. Recently they have sensed a great evil presence coming from right outside the gates of St. Christopher's Academy. The Vatican knew that this was their only time to strike. It could be our only chance to discover the City of Demons. The Vatican have been following you for a very long time, Nicholas. You and your family are connected to it all."

Nicholas looked confused, overwhelmed and angry all in the same moment. Here he had thought Amy was a simple girl going to school away from home. He had imagined she was just like any other sixteen-year-old. Now he saw her quite differently.

"So, why did you talk to me in the first place? If it was all business for you, then why be friends with me?"

Amy kept his gaze. "Most of the secrets regarding Demonio involve your family, and so do the mysteries surrounding the Devil's Crown. There is something about your blood that will open the door to this demonic world."

"So, you never liked me. You were just trying to advance your own agenda." Nicholas looked away. He had no desire to make eye contact with her. His cheeks burned. He had never felt so embarrassed and disappointed before.

Amy stepped closer. "Nicholas, I like you a lot. I never meant to hurt you."

"Thought so." He grinned, trying to look more confident than he felt. "I knew you liked me. Even if you came to St. Christopher's Academy as a demon assassin sent by the Pope himself. I'm no fool, I'm a catch." He winked.

"You're a pig," she stated, as though it was common fact.

"What is this Blackwell family secret, anyways?" Nicholas asked, ignoring her insult.

"That's something we're just going to have to figure out. Part of the reason why I came to Demonio with you was to discover that secret."

They kept traveling through the forest. The scenery hadn't changed in an hour of walking. Everything was dark and gloomy. They hadn't crossed a lake or pond or even seen a simple blossom on any of the trees.

Nicholas started to miss the forest surrounding St. Christopher's Academy. He never thought he would miss something as common as a flower. Nothing was green in this forest; all was only black, grey, and mud brown.

Suddenly, Nicholas felt a prickle across his neck. A voice whispered in his ear causing his body to tingle. *I waited so long for you, great Nicholas Blackwell.* Nicholas looked to Amy, but it was obvious that she had not spoken a word, or heard the voice, so he ignored the whisper. A few minutes later and the singing voice continued. *Strong as a gladiator, braver than a lion. Most handsome man. Nicholas, desired above all. You weaken me, oh Great One.*

"Did you hear that?" Nicholas asked.

"Careful Nicholas, the silence in a forest can play tricks," Amy said. "You may think you hear something, but nothing is there."

"It sounded so real." He pressed his hand against his forehead.

As his fingers combed through his hair, the alluring whisper started again. *I am forever yours, Nicholas. My blood, my body, it belongs to no one but you. Come to me and I promise to fulfill all your deepest desires. Take me, I'm yours.*

Nicholas halted, his eyes glazed over in a trance.

"What's wrong?" Amy asked.

Nicholas didn't answer, but changed direction and started through the forest. Amy trailed after him as he walked with purpose, as though he saw something hidden within the utter darkness that she could not see.

Abruptly, the dirt floor turned into an asphalt driveway. A mansion loomed in the night, surrounded by tall, bare trees. The ebony brick structure was three stories high, surrounded by white pillars. A network of vines covered the walls. Fog wrapped the courtyard, making it hard to see.

"Nicholas, how did you know this was here?" Amy asked.

He didn't respond, but instead continued up the driveway toward the mansion.

An elegant fountain rose out of the courtyard. Two maidens were bathing in it. Soft giggles broke the silence, as the maidens slowly ran their fingers through each other's luscious hair. They ignored the newcomers as they continued their activity. *Can they see us?* Nicholas wondered. He ascended a small staircase to the front porch and opened the massive front doors, stepping onto the black marble floor within.

The mansion was classically exquisite. Stairs curved down both sides of the entrance hall. Extravagant paintings of beasts hung on the walls, lofty windows were covered with thick red drapes, and a collection of small antique sculptures sat in tall glass display cases. An iron chandelier of multicolored stained glass hung down in the foyer, reflecting an array of colors across the entrance. Beneath the chandelier stood a round glass table filled with exotic foods. The smell of rich perfume lingered seductively in the air.

A shirtless man stood in the corner. His hands were entwined around the body of a beautiful woman with long hair cascading down to her lower back in large curls. Her back pressed against the wall, one leg wrapped around the man's waist, her hand against his bulging chest as she giggled softly and whispered in his ear.

"Excuse me," Amy said awkwardly, though the man's and woman's adoring glances and gentle touches to each other showed they didn't hear her.

"I think we might be interrupting," Nicholas told Amy from the side of his mouth. He was ready to step out of the mansion and head for a new destination.

The man's lips parted, revealing large fangs as he touched the girl's neck. He bit into her flesh, his large hands holding onto her waist as he sucked her blood. She flipped her long hair over her shoulders and turned away from him. Her eyelids fluttered weakly and she caught a glimpse of Nicholas and Amy. It took a moment for the girl to focus on them.

"Nicholas Blackwell." Her hand reached out for him. "Would you like to taste me? My blood is sweet and is perfectly aged. Ripe. It would be my honor."

Nicholas gulped, "I'm not really a blood-sucking kind of a guy."

Her hand fell limp at her side. She slid slowly to the floor. The man followed her slumping body, fangs still attached to her neck, still drinking her blood.

She moaned slightly in a combination of pleasure and pain, "I need you, Nicholas. I want you. I desire nothing more."

"Enough with theatrics, Flora."

Nicholas turned to see who had spoken. Walking down the staircase was the most beautiful woman he had ever seen. Her skin was soft and fair, her full lips as red as blood. Long, chocolate brown hair was held up by a ruby-speckled comb. Her body, shaped like an hourglass, swayed elegantly as she glided down the stairs. A skin-tight silky red dress hugged her body. Eyes the color of amethyst found Nicholas and a smile lit up her flawless face.

"Pardon Flora here, she truly is a dramatic child."

Nicholas stepped to the end of the staircase, and held out a hand. The woman took it and kissed his cheek. She gently grabbed his chin and said, "Good boy."

"What's going on?" Amy asked. "Who are you?"

Nicholas was much too stunned by the touch of the woman's soft skin and luscious body to even speak. He was lost in her beauty.

"Hello there," she smiled toward Amy, finally acknowledging her presence.

The woman wrapped her arm around Nicholas, leading him to the round glass table. Her high heels clicked against the marble as she walked. The table was filled with chocolate-dipped strawberries, oysters, gold-wrapped bars of dark chocolate, truffles, and a bottle of red wine. A pyramid of elegant glasses stood beside the wine. "Would any of you care for a glass?"

"No, thank you," Amy said firmly, arms folding across her chest.

The woman smiled. "More for me." She took a chocolate-covered strawberry and bit into it. Nicholas watched the strawberry juice stain her red lips. She poured herself a glass of wine and held it daintily in her fingers.

"Who are you?" Amy demanded.

"Don't you think that's rather rude?" The woman grabbed another strawberry and dipped it into her wine. "After all, you are the one who has entered my home without invitation." As she spoke, she circled the strawberry along the rim of the glass and then raised it to her lips. Nicholas gulped as she bit down on the strawberry this time.

The man in the corner of the room had finally disengaged from Flora's neck. She lay against the marble floor, limp, as if deflated. Content with his meal, he walked barefoot across the room, stopping as he reached the mistress of the house, standing like a dog at her heels.

"Who's my good boy? How was din-din?" she asked as she rubbed his hard, defined stomach.

"Delicious," he answered.

"Good," she smirked, eyes drifting after Amy. "Now how about dessert? Seize her."

"No!" Amy screamed as the man stepped toward her.

With little effort he snatched her wrist and pulled her toward him, forcing her hands behind her back as he held her tightly.

"Nicholas, help me!" Amy cried. But Nicholas had lost his ability to move. He could not take his eyes off the woman by the glass table. "Snap out of it! Nicholas, please," Amy begged.

The woman smiled as she took a sip of her wine. "My name is Marluxia. I am one of the seven Princes. The Guardian of *Lust*."

This snapped Nicholas out of his bedazzlement. "Prince? But you're a woman."

"We were given our title of Prince long before 'Princess' became a word. Before the distinction between a man and a woman even mattered." Marluxia spoke directly to Nicholas, and once again he fell under her spell. "I know all about you, Nicholas, son of Oliver and Kathleen Blackwell. You do have your father's good looks." She bit down on her bottom lip and took Nicholas's hand. The moment they touched, a tingling sensation crawled up his arm and coursed through his body. He craved Marluxia, like a desirable dream.

"Get off of him!" Amy yelled. She squeezed free from the man's grip and pulled a dagger out from a sheath on the man's belt, throwing it at Marluxia. The blade sliced the air grazing Marluxia's impeccable neck.

Marluxia hissed, revealing two fangs. Her face hardened. "What part of 'seize her' do you not understand, you imbecile?"

The man grabbed Amy again, roughly this time. Marluxia laughed, then turned back to Nicholas. "Come to me, my boy."

Nicholas stepped closer and reached for her hand, touching her lightly. "I think I love you. I want to be with you… forever."

She placed her hands on Nicholas's shoulders, running them down his arms. Her touch was pleasant, numbing. "What about your friend?" she asked, her voice reaching him as if from a distance.

"I don't care," Nicholas said dully.

Marluxia smirked. "Do you want to stay here with me, in my mansion, for all eternity?" She looked over Nicholas's shoulder at the struggling Amy.

"Yes."

"Are you more attracted to me than you ever were to that redheaded pest?"

"Yes, her beauty is nothing compared to you."

"Good — now I'm feeling rather hungry."

Nicholas reached for an oyster and placed the shell against Marluxia's lips. She threw back her head as she devoured the oyster. Licking her lips she said, "They say that oysters flame the desire." She ran her finger down Nicholas's neck. "With just one bite," she bit her bottom lip, "your hormones peak." She waved her empty wine glass in front of Nicholas's face. "My glass is empty. But I still thirst." Her fangs sliced into his neck.

Nicholas felt no pain. He stood there as she fed on him, as if oblivious to what Marluxia was doing. Through his daze he could hear Amy's screams as she tried to pull away from the man who held her captive, but he didn't care. Nothing mattered except Marluxia's closeness.

Marluxia moved her wine glass to Nicholas's wound. Blood spilled slowly into the glass and filled it halfway to the top. She raised the glass, laughing. "And now, my brothers, my fellow Guardians of Sin, will drink the sacred blood of our greatly despised enemy, allowing us to rise again to conquer all."

"What do you mean?" Amy asked, her voice reaching Nicholas again.

*Me? Are they talking about me?*

Marluxia waved the glass. "Nicholas's blood is the blood of Innocence. Because of it, we have been weakened. Drinking the blood, consuming its spells, will be our awakening."

Amy bolted, finally pulling free from the slave's grip. She reached forward and grabbed Nicholas's hand, dragging him toward her. He fell against her, and Amy pressed her lips against him, kissing him passionately.

He blinked weakly, as if awakening from a dream. His heart pounded. Before he knew it, he was kissing Amy back, his desire for Marluxia forgotten. His toes curled, blood rushing through his body as the kiss deepened.

"Stop her!" Marluxia ordered and Amy was yanked back, away from Nicholas's touch.

Nicholas gasped, coming back to his senses. Did Amy just kiss him? Of her own will? Was she really attracted to him? The thought made his head spin.

Amy's screams brought Nicholas back to reality. He swept the dagger off the floor and waved it toward Marluxia. She cackled as she carefully placed the glass of his blood onto the round table, then snatched an empty glass and smashed it against the edge of the table holding the broken glass toward Nicholas like a knife.

"What do we do now?" Nicholas asked Amy out of the corner of his mouth.

Amy twisted out of the arms of the man holding him and ran to his side. "The Crown." Her eyes darted around. "Each Guardian's power is fueled by their piece of the Crown. But that piece could be anything."

Marluxia began to circle them, still cackling. "Lust is a powerful sin, and teenage boys are the most easily seduced. I hardly had to try."

"Oh yeah, well I overcame you." Nicholas plunged his dagger into her stomach.

It didn't work as he had hoped. Marluxia's laughter rang through the room. Her hands wrapped around the blade's handle. As she bent to pull the dagger from her stomach, Nicholas caught a better look of the ruby comb placed regally on her head, like a Princess would wear her Crown. *The Crown. Could it be?...* He reached forward and snatched the comb from her hair, crying in agony as the comb burned like scalding water. Nicholas dropped the comb to the floor. Marluxia whipped around, her lips quivering with rage.

"That's got to be it!" Nicholas exclaimed. "The comb is the Crown!"

"Destroy it!" Amy cried out.

Nicholas reached for the comb, but at that moment Marluxia snatched him by the throat, lifting him off the floor.

"You are no match for the power of *lust!*"

Nicholas kicked out at the table beside him and the pyramid of glasses crashed to the floor. The wine bottles spilled all over, as did Marluxia's glass filled with his blood. Marluxia released Nicholas and made a run for the comb. Just as Nicholas's blood touched the comb, Marluxia stopped in her tracks. She screamed.

Her body burst into a spray of black blood and whirled like a tornado, disappearing into the comb. Wind gusted around the room.

Marluxia's screams didn't end until the comb consumed every bit of blood. Once Marluxia vanished, her handsome pet shrank. His body distorted and a guinea pig was left in his place. The tiny pig scurried frantically across the glossy floor.

"One down," Nicholas said, taking the now-cool comb off the marble floor and putting it away in his backpack. "What do we do now?"

"Did you see what your blood did to her?" Amy's voice trembled. "I think we need to speak with Ramiro and Pugdush a little more. They know more than they're telling."

"How about we talk about that kiss first," Nicholas said, leaning in to her and brushing a string of Amy's hair behind her ear.

"How about we never mention it again," she said with a half smile.

## DESTINY OR DEATH

Back into the dark woods they traveled, venturing through the cruel night. The evening was becoming spitefully cold; as though even the night didn't appreciate the strangers in the forest. The wind came up in gusts, pushing across tree branches, causing them to bend and unleash a storm of auburn leaves.

As Amy and Nicholas continued on, hand in hand, shivering silently in the blistering cold, they came across a circle of trees, the only area in the entire woods covered in snow. Together they stepped through the trees and entered a winter meadow. Dead plants with black and violet leaves poked out from the frost and surrounded a chess table. At the table a pair of small demons sat across from each other, having a match. The demons looked like twins, identical except for the position of scars across their milky-white faces. Both had colorless hair, thick as cords, falling down to their shoulders. Their eyes had no pigment in their pupils. Yellowish-white wings behind their backs twitched every so often.

"Check," one demon grunted as he hit the counter box on top of the table.

"Not so fast," the other said, moving his queen clear across the chess board. "Got you again." His smile made him look like a toad.

"Excuse me," Amy said. The two demons turned to face her. "Do you know the way out from these woods?"

"Sometimes," they said as one.

"How do you *sometimes* know?" Nicholas asked.

"Because sometimes we do and sometimes we don't," the demon on the right said as he moved a pawn forward.

"You make no sense," Nicholas said.

"We make *perfect* sense. Paths in these woods only show themselves when they choose to." The demon moved a knight.

"This place is insane." Amy turned away.

"Aren't we all just a bit insane?" the demon said, eyes sparkling madly. "Why, I am the Demon of Destiny and I find myself peculiar all the time."

"You can say that again." The other demon took out his opponent's pawn with his queen.

"I didn't know there was a Demon of Destiny," Amy said. "Just the Angel of Destiny."

The two demons shared a laugh. "You can't expect the Angel of Destiny to guard and protect evil destiny, can you?"

"I guess not," Amy admitted.

"Can't see her tolerating demon affairs," Destiny rasped.

"Why, you might just think there isn't a Demon of Death either," said the demon across from Destiny.

"There is?" Nicholas felt intrigued and frightened at the same time.

"Well, of course there is. After all, I should know who I am, wouldn't you agree?"

"I would hope so," Nicholas agreed.

"So, you two are the Demon of Destiny and the Demon of Death?" Amy asked.

"Looks that way," Death said. "Unlike the Angel of Death, I only take the souls of evil beings."

"What brings you lads to Demonio?" Destiny asked. "You smell like demons, but your looks are suspiciously human."

"Perhaps they came to Demonio to die?" Death grinned.

"I hope not," Nicholas gulped.

"That's a shame." Death sighed. "You two would make a lovely addition to my collection of souls. Would you not agree, Destiny?"

"Indeed."

"You guys are strange," Nicholas said.

Death smiled and cocked his head toward Nicholas. "You're an interesting one, aren't you? Powerful soul. Not many like it." He turned to Destiny. "What do you suppose favors him more, Destiny or Death?"

Destiny shrugged. "Depends if he survives." He turned to Nicholas. "The Guardians of Sin will test you, but if you succeed, perhaps greatness will be your foretelling."

"Or death," Death added.

"Defeating Lust was hardly a challenge. Mind that the Guardians become more difficult as your journey continues," Destiny said.

The trees surrounding the meadow began moving, separating and creating two new paths. The moaning and shrieking as the wind whistled through them made Nicholas and Amy huddle closer together.

"Which path?" Nicholas asked.

Amy pointed to the closest one. It looked as though it led away from the mansion, while the other path appeared to go back toward it.

"Can't go that way," Death said.

"Why not?" Amy asked.

"That path leads to sudden death," Destiny said.

"Wouldn't want you to go down that path." Death shook his head. "I still have a chess match to win."

"Thank you, we'll let you two get on with your game." Amy and Nicholas slowly stepped back away from the table and toward the further path. A sign appeared, nailed to a tree. Again, it read ONWARD in dark red paint.

"It's a shame you're leaving so soon," Destiny said. "I'm winning."

Nicholas and Amy hurried through the woods, away from the demons. Despite moving quickly, jogging, then breaking into a run, they felt cold. Even when they felt they were a safe distance away, the demons' voices still resonated in their thoughts, keeping their flesh crawling.

They had run what seemed a mile without stopping. Nicholas hadn't noticed his breath becoming raspy as he fought for oxygen. Amy too was panting. After a while Nicholas stopped, sinking to his knees. His chest felt as though it carried a strap of bricks and he felt light-headed as he tried to stop his uncontrollable wheezing.

"Use your inhaler," Amy said.

He looked up at her with unfocused eyes. "How did you know?" Humiliation washed over him replacing the fear he'd felt.

"You might put on a good act for the kids at school, but you don't fool me, Nicholas. It's absolutely ridiculous to hide the fact that you are asthmatic. Stop living with your pride and take care of yourself."

Nicholas grabbed his backpack and zipped open the small pouch in the front. He put the inhaler against his trembling lips. With two puffs, his body relaxed. He stood back up with renewed strength.

"You feel better?" Amy asked.

He nodded, still embarrassed.

"No more secrets. If you need your inhaler, use it."

Nicholas met her eyes. "Now you know my secret, tell me yours."

She stepped back. "What do you mean?"

"Why did the Vatican send a teenage girl to Demonio? It doesn't make sense."

Amy looked away. "Because of you."

"What? Why?" He peered into her hesitant face. As much as he wanted to believe she was referring to her attraction to him, he knew better. Her reluctance told him as much.

Amy turned back to him. "Your family has a secret. Like it or not, this secret begins here. More, it intertwines with the Mankind's safety. You're the last living Blackwell, the only one left who can unlock them. The Vatican thought I would be the best candidate for this mission, one who could easily befriend you because we're a similar age."

Nicholas swallowed. "OK. You've befriended me. Now what?"

"Now I will do my best to help you solve your family's secret, so we can save the world."

"What?"

"If we don't weaken the Guardians of Sins, they will reach Humankind and put it in terrible jeopardy. They will unleash the deadly sins, plunging humanity into darkness. Everything that either of us have ever known would be gone."

For a long moment, neither spoke a word. They stood in the unbearable dark forest with only the sound of cracking undergrowth made by unseen creatures that Nicholas didn't want to know about. He thought of his parents, realizing how little he knew about them. *Why didn't they tell me about the Blackwell family secret? Did they die trying to protect it...? Do I want to know what that secret is?* These thoughts gnawed at his mind, sucking away all happy and rational thoughts. His stomach twisted.

"Nicholas, we have to start trusting each other." Amy met his eyes.

Nicholas nodded, turning to continue through the forest. After a while they found the path filled by swirling hookah smoke—the same smoke that had transported them out of Ramiro's bookshop and into the middle of the woods.

Amy hesitated before stepping into the smoke. Nicholas wrapped his fingers around Amy's and smiled as he looked into her eyes. "I'll keep you safe, I promise. Trust me." He wasn't sure where his confidence came from, but he knew he would do everything in his power to keep this promise.

The smoke was blinding as it curled around them. All they could see was a gray sheet. As the smoke slowly pulled apart, they found themselves standing on the glossy redwood floor of the bookshop. They wound their way through the labyrinth of tall bookshelves until they reached the old demon coughing up long rings of smoke.

"You found your way." He grinned. "Interesting, but you are not nearly close to the end. Lust has been weakened, a great Prince has fallen, but six more await who are much stronger than Marluxia." Ramiro brought the hose to his lips and sucked the smoke in from the corner of his mouth. "Lust is nothing compared to the others." Smoke cascaded down his old, leather lips.

"What do you know about Nicholas's blood?" Amy asked. "Marluxia said that if the Guardians drink his blood, it will allow them to conquer the world once again. What did she mean by that?"

"Drinking Nicholas's blood would seal the Guardians' awakening," Ramiro said. "It would make them permanent in the human world. Nicholas's parents have been here before. Instead of containing the Guardians within their piece of the Devil's Crown, your parents, Nicholas, contained them within their unborn child, because your blood was the blood of innocence, the blood of a child that had not yet sinned."

"I've sinned plenty enough since then," Nicholas said.

"It doesn't matter. Your blood will continue to be innocent because it has become the vessel that bound the Guardians within it. It makes them weak, fragile. When you ate the forbidden fruit you created a hole in your innocence that gave them a way out. The Guardians still do not have the strength they once had, so you must challenge them now, before it's too late. Drinking your blood stimulates their talents, but it is also their weakness. Like you just experienced, spilling your blood upon their piece of the Crown imprisons them into it."

"It might have been helpful to have known that before," Nicholas exclaimed. "We almost died back there!"

"Discovering secrets is part of the adventure. You mustn't be handed every little detail, but uncover it for yourself."

"You act like this is just some game," Nicholas said.

"Nothing could be further from the truth." The demon sucked the hookah hose again, though this time no smoke came out. His eyes darted to the coals, reduced to a pile of ash. "Pugdush! More coals!"

The tiny demon scurried out from the back of the shop with a tray of newly heated coals; he placed three pieces on the top of the hookah with tiny metal tongs.

Ramiro pulled smoke into his mouth. "Demonio is very much a reality. The Guardians must be stripped of their power over sin. If all seven Princes drink Nicholas's blood, it would be futile to fight them. The seven deadly sins would rise from Demonio and enter the Mankind's World with renewed power. The end would be inevitable."

"He means the end of humans," Pugdush added, his head bouncing with nods.

"Do you have anything to eat?" Nicholas asked.

Amy's eyes shifted in Nicholas's direction, her nose twitching in distaste.

"What? I'm hungry," Nicholas said defensively.

Pugdush brought out a silver tray of pastries. Nicholas grabbed a handful and dug in. After a hesitation, Amy took one. She eyed Ramiro.

"I doubt your allegiance. Risen demon, you say, but I hesitate to believe it. Demons are easily bored and like to amuse themselves watching the outcomes of adventures, prophecies, anything out of the ordinary."

Ramiro rasped a chuckle, "You have to try harder than that, dear. If it is discovered that I and Pugdush are part of the Risen, I assure you, the best we both would hope for is quick death. Demonio is the gateway to Hell. If exposed, we would be sent to the darkest, cruelest parts of the underworld."

"I'll take another." Nicholas reached for more pastries. He licked the frost off an éclair and then bit down into its creamy center.

Ramiro lifted an eyebrow, lips puckering over the hookah hose. "I don't think you understand how grave your situation is. I can't stress enough what kind of power is entailed with the seven Princes of Hell. It has been centuries since the pieces of the Devil's Crown have been joined as one. The Mankind's World knows not of the demons that it once had. Demon seekers have fought for many years, binding evil within the walls of Demonio, giving demons no freedom to terrorize. And now, I'm afraid Demon Seekers have become scarce and the rise of evil has become more imminent. You, Nicholas Blackwell, are the last hope for salvation."

"You got anything else to eat?" Nicholas asked.

Everyone in the room turned to Nicholas and the empty tray in his lap.

"Can't you think of anything else but your stomach?" Amy sounded both surprised and irritated.

Nicholas sniffed, "I smell something." He sniffed again. "Bacon?"

"Pugdush no cook bacon," Pugdush said.

Ramiro caught Nicholas's eyes. "You feel it, don't you? The next Guardian is near, beckoning you."

"What do you mean?" Amy asked.

"Nicholas is becoming more susceptible to the sins. You mustn't waste time. Your next challenge awaits," Ramiro answered.

Suddenly, the smell of bacon turned to a freshly baked pumpkin pie. The inviting scent became unbearable and Nicholas felt he had no choice but to follow, Amy trailing him outside the store.

Ramiro's shop was only one of many lining the murky streets. Next to it loomed what could have been a pet shop once upon a time. The cages showcased not living creatures, but the skeletons of animals left behind. Amy averted her gaze as she sped past the shop, keeping close to Nicholas.

They curved between brick buildings into a bigger street, with many other winding streets sprouting off it in all directions. The city looked animated and odd, with slanted tall buildings and uneasily sitting homes. Everything looked to be fashioned by nonsense. Chimneys belched thick black clouds into the sky, casting a dark shadow overhead.

They headed down the serpentine street city until they came to the town square infested with creatures. It looked as though stepping into a child's nightmare. Nicholas and Amy froze in place as they watched the chaotic demons. Goblins ran amuck, ogres waving clubs with sharp nails, creatures that looked like animals possessed by demons trotting along with proprietary looks. But the strangest were the true demons, recognizable by their exotic looks that didn't resemble anything Nicholas had seen before.

As they shouldered through the crowds, a demon shaped like a massive hen flapped its short, stubby wings toward Amy, beckoning her to a stand of jewelry.

"Buy some jewelry, won't you dear," the hen squawked. As she spoke, she dropped an egg that fell onto a pile of other cracked, decaying eggs. "I need to feed me chicks."

They ignored the hen and continued on. The hen grabbed an egg and threw it toward them. It splattered onto the street in front, its sticky, black yolk trickling into a sewer drain.

"Me egg!" the hen continued to squawk with feathers ruffled. "Murderers! They killed me egg!"

No one paid notice as Amy and Nicholas hurried past.

Across the town square, a flash momentarily blinded them. When their vision was restored, a little goblin stood in front of them. It had beady black eyes half-hidden behind thick goggles. A camera with a neck strap hung around his bony shoulders. As he saw them watching, he flashed the camera again, and a picture of Nicholas and Amy emerged, dropping into a pile of pictures scattered around him. The little goblin held out his three-fingered hand for payment for his photograph, but they ignored him and continued on.

"This place is crazy," Amy said.

"No kidding," Nicholas agreed.

"Mama, look," a little demon cried, pointing to Amy. His green face looked like melted wax. "Monster!" he screamed. His mom grabbed him up and pulled her demon child down the street in the opposite direction.

As they reached the other side of town, they came across a crowd of demons. Confetti drizzled from the tops of buildings, black balloons were tied to each street lamp, a banner stretched across two shops reading, FESTIVAL OF FEASTS.

Along the sidewalk fold-up tables were filled with food. The closest one held different types of meat, from chicken to alligator. The next table over displayed an assortment of fish, followed by a variety of pastas and pizzas. A table of breads came after a pancake and waffle station. The rows of food seemed endless and continued to grow the longer Nicholas and Amy stood there.

Nicholas hurried to the pasta and pizza table, pushing past a ferret-shaped demon in a trench coat and two goblins with scaly skins and webbed hands and feet. He grabbed a plate and pulled a slice from four different types of pizza, then scooped up a mound of noodles and plopped it onto his plate.

"You really think now is the time to eat?" Amy asked, while Nicholas lifted a slice of pizza to his lips.

"Why not?" He began chewing. "I'm so hungry."

Amy didn't argue as she leaned against a brick wall, her eyes sweeping across the cluster of demons devouring the food, laughing, smirking and acting as fools. Following her gaze, Nicholas saw a massive troll, far down the street. He sat on an extravagant throne, lifting a silver goblet with amber jewels encrusted along the rim. He cheered his guests and gulped down the goblet's contents. Wine poured down his ugly, wide chin. His flabby body bulged with rolls of fat. The troll grunted and grabbed a raw turkey leg from a table beside his throne. Two pigs, wearing rags and standing upright like humans do, scurried to other tables for food and tossed what they brought onto a mountain of food near the troll. As they watched, the troll ripped the skin off the turkey leg and chewed.

Nicholas didn't have time to gape. He hurried further down the street to a table of cheeses. Amy stayed beside him, shouldering through the crowd of passing demons who were devouring everything in sight. Those that couldn't make it to the tables were making do with eating balloons, banners and rocks. One demon in particular that resembled a warthog, was stretching his mouth around a fire hydrant. Nicholas wished he could do the same so he could shove more food into his mouth. He smacked demon hands away and grabbed another block of cheese off the table.

"Nicholas, stop eating," Amy pleaded.

He ignored her, reaching for another piece. Annoyingly, Amy simply wouldn't let him go. She grabbed his shoulder and pulled him away from the table. He tried to push her away, spotting another table with bowls of rice off to the side.

"Will you snap out of it?" Amy pinched him hard on his arm.

"Ouch!" Nicholas squealed.

She grabbed his face and pulled it closer to hers, looking directly into his eyes. "You're becoming susceptible to the sin. The Guardian of Gluttony is nearby."

"How do you know?" Nicholas asked.

Amy pointed to hundreds of demons devouring food down the street. Everyone surrounded the troll who consumed the most. Pigs in tattered clothing hurried to bring the troll more food.

"He has got to be the Guardian," Amy said.

"I agree. That's disgusting," Nicholas said watching the troll folding a whole, round pizza into a taco and biting into it, cheese and tomato sauce smearing across his hairy face.

"You didn't look much better."

Nicholas shook his head. He still felt hungry, but Amy obviously had a point. "Come on." He grabbed her hand and pulled her with him through the crowd to the troll, who cheered his guests with another goblet of wine.

"Welcome, my friends," the troll spoke, chewing. "I, Prince Gullah, share with you my Festival of Feasts!"

The demons cheered.

"Prince Gullah." Nicholas stepped in front of the troll. He looked repulsive, roughly eight feet tall, with knotted brown fur. Stubby horns projected from his forehead and his wide nose was shaped like a massive teardrop.

"Who are you little people?" the troll grunted, lifting a whole chocolate cake to his mouth. He bit down into the creamy frosting, as he looked down at Nicholas and Amy, waiting for a response.

"I'm Amy Glen."

"Nicholas Blackwell."

Gullah choked on the piece of cake. His pig servants halted, trembling, but the troll didn't seem angry, watching Nicholas with curiosity.

"Blackwell?" His smile revealed a row of tooth decay, blackness between each thick tooth. "Why, Nicholas, you must be the son of my greatest foe." His face shifted to his servants. "More food!" he bellowed, voice echoing across the street.

"Fetch the main course," screeched a pig. "Bring forth the fat boy!"

From down the street, a group of pigs carried a cage over their shoulders. In the cage sat a round boy with glasses. He shivered, eyes darting across the street to the sight of all the demons. *Theodore!*

The troll lifted his head, searching through the crowd. "I love the taste of fat boys. Bring me the fat boy!" He slammed a fist against the arm of his throne.

"Theodore!" Nicholas fought to push through the crowd toward the cage.

Theodore heard Nicholas's voice and gripped the bars, searching through the crowd until he finally spotted him. "Nicholas, help!" he shouted.

The group of pigs dropped Theodore beside Gullah.

Nicholas and Amy broke through the crowd and hurried to the cage.

"How did you get here?" Amy asked.

Theodore wiped his sweaty face with his sleeve and adjusted his bent glasses. "You two left me alone in the bookstore.

I went looking for you around the shops for hours. I was so hungry. Then I found a cheesecake on the floor. I went to pick it up, but it was a trap!" He whimpered as he saw the demons clustered around Gullah. "I want to go home!"

Gullah waved his hand toward Theodore. In a blink, the boy shifted shape, changing into another pig servant. He was still wearing St. Christopher's Academy uniform and broken glasses. He let out a terrified squeal and ran frantically around his cage, before bumping into the bars and knocking himself out.

"Change him back!" Nicholas demanded.

Gullah chuckled, "He has what you call, an "annoying voice." I prefer him this way. There will be no changing him back."

Amy stepped toward Gullah. "Hand over your piece of the Crown and we'll leave you be," she ordered.

The massive face cocked toward Amy. Round, orange eyes, the size of a human head slowly settled on her. "What are you? Demon, you're not; human, I doubt. So, what are you?"

"Hand over your piece of the Crown," she repeated.

Nicholas squinted at Amy, wondering what secrets she might have. She obviously knew more than she let on.

A circle of demons snickered. Gullah tightened his clench on his goblet. Nicholas noticed the movement. *The goblet is the piece of the Devil's Crown.* He wasn't sure how he knew, but he was certain of it.

"What makes you think, little girl, that you can challenge a Guardian of Sin?" Gullah laughed. "I am more powerful than your tiny brain can comprehend."

"Your fellow Prince thought so, too," Nicholas smirked. "Marluxia was much weaker than I thought."

"Lies!" The troll slammed his fist against the arm of his throne. The pig servants scurried behind the table of food, shivering together.

"Afraid not," Nicholas said. "Easy as pie."

The troll rose from his throne and stepped forward, the ground rumbling with every step he took. His hands clenched into fists. Nicholas and Amy edged back, demons around them scurrying out of the away. Gullah seized a bowl of mashed potatoes and poured it into his mouth as if it was the end milk in a cereal bowl. He tossed the useless bowl against a brick wall, shattering it into pieces.

"You foolish children have no idea what you have provoked." He grabbed a lamp post and with little effort yanked it from the concrete. "War." He swung the lamp post like a sword.

Nicholas and Amy jumped out of the way just as the weapon smacked onto the cobbled street. Gullah swung again, this time straight at Nicholas. Nicholas ducked, barely dodging the attack.

"Amy, go get the goblet!" He pointed at the throne, then pushed over a table of fish. A wave of dead sea life poured down the street. Gullah picked up fish-heads and tossed them into his mouth. Nicholas darted toward another table to tip over, but Gullah ran after him, swatting him with an open hand, sending Nicholas slamming into the ground. Nicholas landed roughly, tumbling, ripping his school uniform.

Winded, he watched Amy reach the throne. Three pigs blocked her path, climbing on top of one another so that they towered over the girl. The pig on top pointed its tubby paw toward her. "You cannot pass," he squealed. "That piece of the Crown belongs to none other than the brilliant, stupendous, magnificent Prince Gullah!"

From behind the three pigs, Pugdush appeared on top of the throne. He held a finger up to his lips, then leaned over, snatched the goblet and disappeared.

Nicholas felt someone grip him across the waist, lifting him higher into the air. *Gullah.* "Let me go!" he rasped.

Amy whipped around, her eyes wide. The crowd of demons laughed.

"This is the famous Blackwell son?" Gullah roared. "Descendent of the great and powerful defenders of the Divine? Boy, you're no match for sin!" He tossed Nicholas up into the air.

As Nicholas tumbled in midair thinking this was it, Pugdush appeared on his leg. Wind lashed against his fur as the little demon smiled at Nicholas. "Hang on." Pugdush grasped on as they descended, but just as Nicholas braced for hitting the street, he felt an odd pulling sensation. Instead of smashing into the street, which should have broken all his bones and likely killed him, he found himself standing next to Amy, Pugdush at his side.

Gullah roared. "What magic is this!" He slammed his foot against the street.

Pugdush handed the goblet to Nicholas. It felt hot, burning, but Nicholas kept a tight grip, ignoring the pain. Pugdush slipped him a blade and Nicholas sliced across his hand, then wrapped it around the stem of the goblet. Just as Nicholas's blood touched the goblet, Gullah's knees buckled and he collapsed, giving a mighty roar as his body burst into vomit and soared, pouring into the goblet and out of sight.

All the demons along the cobblestone street paused, then went on their way as if nothing unusual had happened. Nicholas and Amy looked at each other.

"Two down, five to go," Nicholas cheered, with a cocky smile.

Amy turned to Pugdush who looked just as happy as they were. "Pugdush, why did you save us?"

"Pugdush wants to help Nicholas and Miss Amy."

Nicholas made his way over to Theodore's cage. Still a pig, his roommate lay still, unconscious. "What do we do with him?"

Pugdush wrinkled his nose and Theodore disappeared. "Pugdush sent him to Chapel of Dreams. Nicholas's friend be safe for now."

## SOULS FOR SALE

Nicholas, Amy and Pugdush continued on along the main street into the dark city. Most of the demons were gone, leaving the streets nearly empty. Nicholas gazed into the black, murky sky. It looked so desolate here in Demonio, where not a single star or even the moon welcomed the night. Light was scarce. Amy had mentioned how much she missed sunshine or even a well-lit room, but to his surprise Nicholas didn't share this feeling. The darkness seemed strangely soothing—creepy and chilling, but also oddly peaceful. He wondered why he didn't miss the sun. What was it about him that enjoyed darkness?

"Thanks for saving us," Nicholas said to the little demon.

"Pugdush happy to help." The demon smiled proudly. "Ramiro sent Pugdush to escort Nicholas and Amy. Ramiro offered assistance. Pugdush don't like being Ramiro's apprentice. Pugdush want to go with you two. Pugdush want adventure."

"If you don't like being at the bookshop, why not go up to the Mankind's World?" Nicholas asked.

"Though Pugdush is a Risen demon, Pugdush a demon all the same. The Mankind's World is untouchable by demons. Your sunlight burns us and forces us to stay hidden. Your world only opens to us at 3 a.m. and that is the only time we may leave Demonio, but if demons aren't back to Demonio by sunrise, we burst into flames and are sent straight to Hell. Long ago, when the Guardians of Sin were at their peak of domination, their power would shield the sun and allow demons in the Mankind's World whenever demons wished. These were dark times, terribly dark times."

"Interesting," Nicholas said. "So, no Risen demon has ever made it out of Demonio forever?"

"No," Amy said. "A Risen demon can only do it if he proves himself worthy of the Light."

"How the heck do you know all that? Did you learn about Risen demons in the Vatican?" Nicholas demanded.

Amy averted her eyes but didn't say anything.

"Sure, don't tell me. Who cares? Not like we're facing sudden death, challenging the greatest horrors in the world. Let me die without learning any of your secrets."

Amy laughed, but didn't say anything.

As they continued down the street, they heard loud noises coming from an oval-shaped building. They went to investigate. A rhino-looking demon in a striped suit, red tie and a hat that resembled something a mobster would wear, stood guard at the entrance.

"Don't bother going in there," Pugdush assured them. "Just demon affairs. The Guardians won't be there."

"Maybe we can get information about where the next Guardian is," Nicholas suggested.

Amy nodded.

"Okay, but Pugdush warn you, what you may see in there won't be pretty."

"Nothing in this place has been pretty," Amy said, glancing around at their gloomy surroundings.

"Alright, but remember, Pugdush warned you."

Together, the three walked up to the rhino. He studied them with a probing eye.

"Three going in," Pugdush announced.

"Suit yourself." The rhino held out a leathery hand. "One junk from each of you."

Pugdush reached into his cloak pocket and handed over a string of dental floss, a button and a used band-aid.

The rhino-like demon examined each piece. He held the button up and squinted to make sure it was real. He sniffed the junk and scratched the side of his horn. "Alright, these will do." He opened the door and allowed them to enter. "Your room number is six."

Pugdush led the way through a narrow hallway, curving alongside the building, beneath a dome-shaped roof.

"Is this how demons pay for things? With junk?" Nicholas asked. "Cause we can just go back to my room and I can find us enough junk to buy ourselves Marluxia's mansion."

Amy rolled her eyes.

"Payment is usually made through junk that is found in the Mankind's World. But it must be authentic. Junk must still have human stench." Pugdush pointed to the ceiling. "Though demons do prefer gold for the big ticket items like mansions."

They reached room six. Pugdush jumped for the door knob and twisted. Nicholas assisted by pushing the door open. They entered a gloomy room with three red-cushioned chairs beside a tinted glass window. The walls were painted black. A single lamp did little to illuminate the rest of the room. Pugdush jumped into the middle chair and Nicholas and Amy took the ones beside him. Next to each chair was a microphone with a red button, a number carved into its middle. A speaker sat near the button. Nicholas's number was twelve.

"What's going on?" Amy asked. She looked out of the tinted window to see that all the rooms throughout the building had windows facing the center.

"Just watch," Pugdush said. "Don't be emotional. Close yourself off. It's your only chance of surviving what happens here."

"I don't think coming here was a good idea," Nicholas said.

"What may happen?" Amy asked.

Just then, a light in the center of the building beamed on. Nicholas's eyes swept across all the tinted windows of rooms nearby that he could not see into. Chills ran down his spine as he imagined what sort of demons could be hidden behind each black glass panel.

A man in a heavy coat entered the room in the center of the building. He walked up to the very center so that everyone behind the tinted glass windows could see him. As he turned Nicholas's way, a surge of terror crashed into him like a wave against rocks. His face pinched, and he clenched his jaw.

He was staring into the eyes of his parents' murderer.

"Welcome, everyone," the man shouted, "to *Souls for Sale*. For those of you who don't know me, I am Romulus Urdermay, the owner of this establishment. I thank you all for joining me today. The bidding starts immediately. For any newcomers, bids are placed by pushing the red button beside you. The highest bid wins the prize. Simple as that. Now, let's begin."

Another man entered, this one in overalls. Nicholas remembered him as the man that had eaten all his Christmas cookies. He placed a closed cardboard box in the middle of the room.

"What's in there?" Amy gripped the arms of her chair, her eyes glued to the box.

A litter of spotted puppies poked their heads out from the box. Their paws were hanging over the flaps in desperate attempts to escape.

Amy covered her mouth. "Oh my God, what are they going to do to them…? What is this place?"

"*Souls for Sale*," Pugdush reminded her. "I told you it wouldn't be pretty. You've seen nothing yet."

Romulus stood beside the box of puppies. "Now, these newborns would make a lovely vessel for your demonic soul. Perfect age. Won't put up a fight."

"Oh, God." Amy buried her face in her hands.

Romulus grabbed a puppy by the skin on the back of its neck and lifted it up. The puppy licked Romulus's hand as he was showcased to the audience.

"As you all know, puppies make fine vessels. They are easily corrupted and can be morphed into your darkest desires. Their stupidity and loyalty will simplify the possession. We'll start the bidding at twenty junks."

Through the microphone, a chilling voice announced, "Twenty-five." A moment later a rough, ragged voice bid higher. The voices announcing the numbers made Nicholas's skin curl; it sounded like the stuff of nightmares. The bidding stopped at thirty-six junks and the auction was over.

The demon in the overalls grabbed the box and carried the puppies away. Shortly after, he brought out a black cat.

"Please, make it stop," Amy pleaded.

Romulus seized the cat and held it out, walking in a circle so that everyone could see. "Now, with Halloween quickly approaching, a black cat could make a lovely ingredient to a cauldron's cocktail. Let's start the bidding at fifty-five junks."

Amy cupped her ears as the cat meowed into the microphone.

"Sixty-four," offered the same chilling voice again.

"One hundred and thirty-eight junks," a raspy voice called.

"Must be a witch I hear." Romulus chuckled happily. "No other bids? No one? Going once, going twice… going three times. Sold!"

The black cat was taken away.

"And now for the more extravagant purchases." The man in the overalls brought in a little boy wearing a metal collar with red chafe marks along his neck. He was pushed to Romulus's side, where he stood, trembling. "This young boy was claimed by the Demon of Wishes," Romulus announced. "Son of Mr. and Mrs. Watson. Brother of two sisters, Emily and Marisa. Mrs. Watson met the Demon of Wishes at the bedside of her dying husband." He stopped for a moment to laugh. "She accepted an offer. The Demon of Wishes would heal her husband in exchange for the soul of her firstborn son. As hard as she tried not to conceive again, Alexander here was born. Only four years old, Alexander would make a fine slave. Young enough to forget his human life and with proper upbringing, he will learn to be loyal. Let's start the bid at one piece of gold."

Quickly, the bids began, numbers climbing higher than all of the previous auctions.

Nicholas watched the boy, tears dripping down his face. He thought of himself when he was seven, when his parents were murdered. He couldn't stand this anymore.

He pushed the red button beside him and spoke into the microphone, "Two hundred gold coins."

Amy and Pugdush quickly turned to him.

"What you doing?" Pugdush yelped. "Do not meddle."

"Two hundred and fifty," offered a cold voice.

"You don't have any gold," Amy reminded.

"I don't care," Nicholas said. He pushed the button again. "Three hundred gold."

Romulus smiled. "Sounds like a new client. Alright then, three hundred gold going once... twice... sold to number twelve!"

Pugdush jumped out of his chair and faced Nicholas. "How you going to pay for that boy? If you don't have the gold, they will punish. Death is mercy in Demonio."

"Where do you get gold here?" Nicholas asked.

"Only at Demonio's City Vault," Pugdush answered.

"Then, let's get going."

 # THE VAULT

Nicholas hurried out of the oval-shaped building. He rushed down the street, staring unseeingly ahead, his teeth clenched so hard that his jaw hurt.

"This way, this way!" Pugdush waved toward the side street.

Nicholas nodded and turned at full speed, skidding around the corner and leveling up with Pugdush. "That demon in there. The one selling the souls. He killed my parents."

Pugdush's eyes narrowed. "Romulus. Menacing demon. Pugdush sorry. Pugdush wish he could help. Pugdush hate sinister demon. Romulus is what you might call a human avatar. He possess a human body, but the true demon lies within."

Amy placed a hand on his arm. "I'm so sorry, Nicholas."

Nicholas wiped his eyes, embarrassed and ashamed. He couldn't remember the last time he'd cried, especially in public, and he refused to do it now.

"Let's just kill these Guardian bastards," he said. "As soon as we're done with the Vault."

Pugdush pointed to a building up ahead. The structure gleamed with a yellow metallic sheen, as if constructed of melted gold. There were no windows along the walls, only a door. Nicholas crossed the street.

Amy hurried after him, once again putting a hand on his

arm. "Nicholas, I want just as much as you to free that boy's soul. But how are you expecting to withdraw gold?"

"I'll think of something."

She closed her grip, pulling him to a stop. "Nicholas. You shouldn't interfere. There are certain consequences for human actions. The boy's mother made an unbreakable deal."

Nicholas whipped around. "How do you know, Amy, that the deal that boy's mother made was unbreakable?"

She hesitated. "I just know."

"How?" he insisted. "I don't think the Vatican knows that much about deals made by demons. Besides, that boy should not have to pay for his mother's mistake. I'm getting him out of there, no matter what the cost."

Pugdush shook his head vigorously. "The only way to get gold without proper trade, is to steal from the Vault."

Amy frowned. "Can we?"

"We try," Pugdush said.

They ascended the steps and pushed through a revolving door into a giant room. Nicholas slowly walked forward. Wooden floorboards creaked underfoot. Along the walls, mountains of junk rose to the high ceiling, receding into the deep shadows. Nicholas gaped. Anything and everything he had ever thought useless was scattered around the room: broken pencils, old bikes, dirty clothes, ripped curtains, old toothbrushes, guitars with missing strings, cracked china, and countless other items. Stale smells of rot and dust filled the air.

The demons' Vault was no more than a giant garbage pile. Everything that could be found in trash cans, cluttered attics, or landfills comprised the demons' currency.

A demon Nicholas guessed to be a bank teller sat on a nearby counter top. He resembled a very sick rabbit with tall, bent ears twisting in odd directions. It seemed that he couldn't sit still even for a second as he constantly twitched and scratched his ears, as if fighting an endless battle against his fleas. One of his feet was missing, replaced with a wooden stick.

"Welcome to the Demonio City Vault," he said through a mouth full of tiny carrot chunks. "What do you want?"

"We came for gold," Pugdush said.

"To steal or purchase?"

"Steal."

"Right this way then." The rabbit-demon jumped off the counter and led the way through the bank. Gnawing on a carrot, he opened a pair of swinging doors in the far back into a narrow hallway with a low ceiling. Nicholas hunched over, his head skimming against the ceiling.

"*Thisssss way.*" Nicholas turned in time to see a snake tail disappearing into a rat hole. He ran after it and knelt down, peeking through the hole. Staring back at him was a slit eye. "*Keep going, Nicholas. You are coming closer to uncovering the secret.*"

"What secret?" Nicholas asked.

"*The Blackwell family secret.*"

Nicholas's hand launched through the hole. The wall above the hole cracked and crumbled away like dirt, creating an opening in the shape of a door. Nicholas stepped through.

It was possibly the dustiest room Nicholas had ever seen. Thick clouds stirred as he entered. Beautiful sheets of cobwebs strung delicately across the hollow space, concealing its true size. Nicholas ducked his head and swooped past, trying not to disturb the hairy spiders crawling up and down their designs. A few webs collapsed at Nicholas's touch, sticking to his hands and clothing.

He stopped as he reached a far wall, facing a low shelf filled with books and boxes too dirty to read. His hand wiped against a box on the top, coming away covered in smoky residue. To his surprise the box read, *Nicholas Blackwell.*

He grabbed the box and took it to the floor. More dust stirred, rising up in wisps as the box hit the ground.

He coughed as he took off the lid and tossed it aside.

Inside were video games, stuffed animals, clothes, action figures, and a superhero nightlight. Everything he left behind when he was taken away to St. Christopher's Academy.

"How is this possible?" Nicholas thought out loud.

*"The archives, discover the truth. The secret's hidden there."*

Nicholas stood up. He didn't know why he suddenly felt like he had to move the bookshelf over. He had no reason to believe something was hidden there. He moved it anyway. There, behind the bookshelf, was a painting of a dead tree with names on each branch. Above the tree an elegant inscription read, *The Blackwell Family Tree.*

Nicholas ran his eyes down the list of names.

Liam Blackwell
Oliver Blackwell
Nicolas Blackwell
Gavin Blackwell

Laurence Blackwell
Isaac Blackwell
V. Blackwell
Elson Blackwell

Timothy Blackwell
Huxley Blackwell
E. Blackwell

Dustin Blackwell
Everhart Blackwell
Vincent Blackwell
Isadore Blackwell
L. Blackwell

Nicholas read again, wondering about the spaces between the groups of names, and the way the first letter of each name was written in a bolder script, different from the rest of the line. Inadvertently, he started reading these letters alone, top to bottom. As he reached the end, he stepped back, feeling his entire body seized with chill.

The first initials of each name spelled a phrase of their own.

**LONG LIVE THE DEVIL**

Panicked, he stepped back and tripped over the box on the floor, tumbling down and hitting his head on a chipped stone. He sat up and pressed his hand to his forehead. Blood oozed between his fingers.

A bright yellow snake slithered past his feet, hissing. Another snake, this one as black as night, with silver markings, glided over his hand. He forced himself to his knees, back to the bookshelf.

"I'm not afraid of you, I'm not afraid of you," he muttered over and over again.

Snakes dropped from the top of the bookshelf, scattering around him quickly. He closed his eyes, panting hard, chest about to explode. His shaking hands searched for his inhaler, dropping it several times before it finally reached his lips. Three puffs, eyes clenched. Breathing became easier. He could feel a number of the snakes against his skin.

"Stop it, go away!" he screamed.

Suddenly he couldn't feel the snakes anymore. He opened his eyes and all the snakes were gone.

He jumped to his feet, wiping his hands on his shirt, and rushed back into the hallway.

"Nicholas!" Amy hurried toward him, Pugdush and the bank teller right beside her. "Are you all right?"

He nodded.

"You're trembling."

"I'm fine. Let's go."

Without another word, Nicholas followed the bank teller. After a long walk down the narrow hallway, they came to a broad iron door with four locks. The bank teller grabbed a ring of keys and unlocked each lock separately. With a great push, he forced the door open.

"I can't go beyond here. You three will now be on your own," he said.

Shoulder to shoulder, Nicholas and Amy entered the room with Pugdush at their heels.

Everything here seemed to be made of gold: the floor, the walls, piles of bars and coins, even the tapestries. A water fountain in the center of the room gushed out glittering golden water. In the back of the room, on a mountain of coins, lay a leprechaun. He was using an enormous diamond as a pillow for his large head, his lipless mouth drooling a creamy liquid. His eyes crossed as he looked at the three strangers.

"You!" he shouted, pointing a long, thin finger toward Nicholas. His nails were sharp, with each finger bearing a jeweled ring.

The leprechaun made a move to rise, but fell back, as if unable to move.

"What's wrong with him?" Nicholas asked.

Pugdush shrugged. "Don't know."

"You did this to me!" the leprechaun said. "You can't have it. It's mine, all mine." He pulled piles of gold into his arms, shaking pathetically.

"Who are you?" Amy asked.

The leprechaun coughed a spray of cream, "I am Avarice, Guardian of Greed, a Prince of Hell."

"You weakened him," Pugdush told Nicholas.

"I didn't touch him."

"The boy you wanted to save, you came here to get gold to free his soul. You did charity."

"It isn't Nicholas's gold to give," Amy pointed out.

"But he never meant to keep it. That's charity, one of the seven virtues. The opposite of greed."

"Charity, my final adversary," Avarice grunted. "It's mine." He crawled toward his treasure, pulling mounds of coins into his arms, holding them tightly to his chest. "It's all mine, you can't have it. You mustn't. It's all mine. Mine. Mine!"

"Where is your piece of the Devil's Crown?" Amy asked.

"You speak rubbish! I have no piece of the Crown."

Nicholas noticed Avarice clenching a golden hand and pointed. Amy nodded and climbed the mountain of coins to reach for it.

"It's mine. All mine!" With full force, Avarice struck Amy's arm with his golden hand. Slowly a golden wave seized Amy's arm, starting at her elbow and ending at her fingertips. She screamed and tumbled back, her arm turned to gold. Nicholas ran to her side.

"The hand Prince Avarice holds turns anything it touches to gold," Pugdush said.

"I want her arm!" Avarice grunted.

Amy lifted her heavy golden arm, holding it up with her free hand. She sobbed.

Nicholas clenched his teeth and rushed up the mountain of gold, coins sliding down beside him in small avalanches.

"Change her arm back!" he demanded.

Avarice drew away, cradling the gold hand. "Get away from me, Nicholas Blackwell!"

Nicholas swallowed. How was it that every demon here seemed to know his name? His skin crept as he remembered the dusty side room.

He leaned over and whispered so that only Avarice could hear his words. "Why do you have a room filled with boxes holding my stuff? And why do you have a family tree of the Blackwells?"

Avarice chuckled, green spit sprayed out from his mouth. "You have no idea who you are?"

"What do you mean?"

Avarice smiled wickedly, "Your bloodline can be traced to your very first ancestor."

"Tell me."

Avarice's eyes widened, his mouth falling open stupidly. His purple tongue twisted as though an invisible hand was tugging at it. He spoke, as if driven by an invisible force. "Your family has a secret known not to any of you, but only to the Princes. Every one of the Blackwells has been watched. Each of their lives ended in a horrible death." Avarice opened and closed his mouth, as if trying to stop talking, but his mouth reopened and he continued. "Every child was born a male, to keep the Blackwell name from becoming lost."

Avarice snapped his mouth shut and covered it with his hand. His eyes shone with defiance as he searched around, fixing his gaze on the bleeding cut on Nicholas's forehead. His lips twisted. "I'd rather die than tell you more!" He reached up and swiped his fingers through Nicholas's blood, then wrapped them around the golden hand.

He screamed as his body burst into a shower of liquid gold, whirling and melding into the leprechaun's piece of the Crown. The golden hand melted, leaving behind a metallic stain.

"Dammit!" Nicholas yelled. He grabbed the Crown piece and shoved it into his backpack, then slid down the mountain of treasure, landing beside Amy and Pugdush.

Pugdush looked up at Nicholas, eyes glistening. "Great warrior. Slayer of demons." He bowed, collapsing to his knees, kissing Nicholas's feet over and over again.

Nicholas slowly relaxed his shoulders, watching the gold in Amy's arm drip away until only her skin was left. Another Guardian defeated. They were getting closer to their goal. But why would Avarice choose to die rather than tell him the secret of his family? He suppressed a shiver, hoisting his backpack up on his shoulder.

"Are you all right?" he asked Amy.

She nodded, looking dazed.

"Good. Pugdush, grab enough coins to cover the boy's cost. And please stop groveling."

## THE PUMPKIN YARD

With enough gold to pay their debt, they left the Vault and headed back to the oval-shaped building. Nicholas couldn't stop thinking about the things Avarice had been about to tell him. *Why did the leprechaun talk, when he obviously did not want to? What secret was he hiding that would be worth dying for?* He forced the questions out of his mind. He had other things to worry about. Not only did he want to free that little boy's soul, but he also now knew where his parents' murderer was. He wasn't sure how, but he was going to have his much-anticipated revenge.

They stopped in front of the building, a few yards away from the rhino-demon guard.

"I want to do this alone," Nicholas announced.

"Nicholas, we're a team, you can't do this alone," Amy protested.

"Nicholas mad at Pugdush?" the little demon asked.

Nicholas shook his head. "You two have been great, but this is something I just have to do myself. Please understand."

"Pugdush trusts Nicholas to be okay. Miraculous warrior, the conqueror of monsters."

Amy hesitated, then nodded.

"Thanks, guys. Stay put. I'll be right back."

Nicholas passed the rhino who merely nodded and stood aside, apparently remembering him from before. He entered the curving hallway, his backpack heavy with gold and the three pieces of the Crown. For a quick second he thought of all the things he could do with the treasure he carried. He could leave school, live on his own, maybe buy a nice apartment. He could probably buy a mansion with just a portion of these coins, and still have plenty left over. Or maybe he could move back to New York City? Nicholas dismissed the thought. Rescuing the little boy was the right thing to do. His father would have done the same thing.

Down the hall, the man in the overalls stood holding a basket of cookies, tossing them into his mouth. Nicholas's mouth twitched with hatred as memories floated into his head. This man, eating his Christmas cookies while laughing at his parent's suffering.

"Picking up your purchase?" the man asked. He tossed another cookie into his mouth.

Nicholas nodded. "Yes. Where is Romulus Urdermay?"

The man in the overalls pointed to a nearby door. Nicholas opened it and entered a lounge with a shaggy red carpet and painted black walls. The smell of liquor lingered unpleasantly in the air. Demons of all sorts were milling around the room. Most were goblins and smaller trolls, and creatures that looked like demonic animals. Some held martini glasses filled with thick red liquid that looked like blood, others nibbled on snacks of tiny insects and beetles from the table. The demons laughed and made faces at each other, like children in a play yard.

Nicholas spotted Romulus leaning against the tinted glass window, with a cigar in his mouth and gorgeous women in skimpy dresses clinging to him on all sides. The demon lifted his head when he saw Nicholas approach.

"Number twelve. Excuse me, girls." He brushed past the girls and stepped forward to meet Nicholas. "Gold?" He took another puff from his cigar.

"Three hundred, as promised." Nicholas dropped his backpack onto the carpet and poured out the coins.

"Wish all my transactions ran this smoothly." Romulus smirked. "Tell me, number twelve, did you steal this gold? Not that I care."

"I know where you can get a lot more," Nicholas prompted.

Romulus lifted one eyebrow and squinted, blowing a thick cloud of smoke in Nicholas's face. "What's in it for you?"

"You look like a demon who appreciates the good life."

Romulus laughed. "Fair enough. So do you."

Nicholas smirked knowingly. "Just hand me over my slave's soul and I'll take you there. Free of charge. No strings attached."

Romulus reached into his pocket and pulled out a small crystal sphere glowing like a shinning star. "Here you go." He handed the sphere over. "Should make a decent slave."

Nicholas took the sphere carefully and put it away. "Follow me."

He led Romulus through the curving hallway, passing the demon in the overalls who continued indulging in cookies.

"You don't remember me, do you?" Nicholas asked.

"Should I?"

"Do Oliver and Kathleen Blackwell ring any bells?"

Romulus halted.

Nicholas met his eyes. "Nine years ago, in the Mankind's World, you murdered my parents without remorse."

Romulus smirked. "Nicholas Blackwell. So you're the Blackwell brat who got away. If that damn angel hadn't rescued you, the Guardians of Sin would have awakened long ago."

"Angel?"

"You're so stupid. You know nothing. I wasn't there to kill you."

Before Romulus could continue, a mighty serpent arose from the shadows. Romulus paled and shrank away as the serpent opened its mouth impossibly wide, slowly devouring Romulus. The demon only had a chance to scream once before disappearing into the serpent's belly.

Nicholas froze, terrified. *Will I be next?* Entranced, he watched the serpent coil down to the floor, its massive head towering over Nicholas.

"Why… did you… do that?" Nicholas forced the words out.

A forked tongue poked out from the snake's lipless mouth. *"What do you know of the Blackwell family secret?"*

Anger drove away Nicholas's fear. "I might have found out if you hadn't eaten my one lead."

The serpent hissed, whipping its neck forward. Its lower body enlarged with the outline of Romulus. *"Stupid boy."*

"Why does everyone keep calling me stupid?"

*"You know not of the legacy. Your birthright is lost on your insignificant life. A great disappointment."* The snake slithered away past Nicholas. Nicholas hurried after it.

Quickly, the serpent moved through the city. Nicholas had to run to keep up. Amy and Pugdush spotted him and hurried to catch up. The serpent bent and shrank to a normal size, its face twisted back toward Nicholas with a wicked smirk. It slid into a sewer drain, and Nicholas darted after it, but the serpent was already at the bottom and out of sight.

Nicholas glanced at Amy and Pugdush who had just caught up. "We need to go after it."

"No following the Great Serpent," Pugdush interjected. "Foolish, stupid, careless boy. Think only with inner pride."

"The snake knows something. We're supposed to follow it. I just know it… And will you demons please stop calling me stupid?"

Pugdush stomped the ground. "Pugdush *not* demon, Pugdush *Risen* demon."

"Last time you followed the serpent it led us here to Demonio," Amy reminded Nicholas.

"It feels like a game," Nicholas said. "I think we have to keep going. Help me break into that sewer."

"We can't just shrink," Amy remarked.

"Pugdush have little magic. Pugdush can make humans small."

"That's great!" Nicholas said.

"But Pugdush won't help reckless boy. The path you follow, Nicholas, leads to your death." The demon folded his arms and stuck his nose in the air.

"I'll get you junk when this is all over," Nicholas promised.

"Pugdush no care for junk. Pugdush likes only one thing more than anything. The most scrumptious of all scrumptiousness. Chocolate."

"I'll get you enough chocolate to last you a lifetime."

Pugdush's face softened. Without another word, he pinched Nicholas on the arm. Nicholas yelped, rubbing the red mark. The more he rubbed the faster he shrank. Everything looked bigger until Pugdush was now a giant and Amy even bigger, her face barely visible high above. Nicholas stopped rubbing. He was probably no bigger than an insect.

Pugdush stepped over Nicholas who ran out of the way as Pugdush's massive foot pounded the ground next to him. A moment later, Amy was rubbing her arm as she shrank, dropping to Nicholas's size. Pugdush joined them soon after.

Nicholas grabbed Amy's wrist and pulled her to the sewer drain. Now of a similar height, Pugdush jogged after them.

"That was some magic," Nicholas said.

"Pugdush don't like using magic. Magic evil. Magic wicked. Magic seductive. Corrupts Pugdush's mind, welcoming evil thoughts."

"How do we get down?" Amy looked into the mouth of the sewer. Shrouded in darkness, the opening was right before them.

Nicholas took out the crystal sphere. The soul's glow shone brightly, creating a dome of light around them. Nicholas spotted a long ladder along the wall, with tiny rungs, as if custom-made for their reduced size. He started descending, one hand on the metal bars, the other holding the sphere to illuminate the way.

Once the ground was close enough, Nicholas jumped and landed on a cement walkway. A potent odor of mildew made him feel nauseated. He held the crystal sphere up and helped Amy down, then Pugdush. Standing shoulder to shoulder with Amy, Nicholas waved the sphere, light wilting the darkness a short distance around them. A black river ran past their feet, a narrow, slippery path running beside it. They walked cautiously down the path.

"Do you think it is wise to follow the serpent, now that we're the perfect size to fit into its mouth?" Amy asked.

"No," Pugdush said quickly.

"If it wanted to eat us, it would have already," Nicholas said.

Dozens of bats, that seemed to Nicholas and his friends to be of an enormous size, flew overhead, the sweep of their wings causing wind to lash against them, slowing their pace. Then, a new sound of something huge moving through the water halted the bat's screeching. Water splashed onto the stone, crashing against their knees. Pugdush squeaked and darted up Nicholas's back and onto his shoulders, fingers gripping Nicholas's face.

"I can't see," Nicholas said, pushing the tiny, hairy hands away.

"Be quiet," Pugdush whispered.

Another wave crashed over the stone, sweeping them over into the dark water. Drenched, they swam with the current, trying to stay near one another.

After a while the current began to shift. Something big was coming. Struggling to stay afloat, Nicholas held up the sphere, light shining further down the sewer. A massive, scaly ship glided across the water, coming his way. As it came closer, Nicholas realized it was not a ship at all. An alligator. Jagged teeth lined its massive jaws, yellow eyes sparkling like fireflies. Nicholas dove into a wave, kicking through the thick water. His shoes and clothes weighed him down, making swimming difficult even for a captain of the swim team. He flipped underwater as the massive body moved next to him. As he pushed in the direction he thought was up, he hit the stone floor. Nicholas kicked off, shooting upward until his head broke through the surface. He gasped, taking deep breaths of much-needed oxygen. When he opened his eyes, he wished he hadn't. The alligator glared down on him, its jagged teeth only feet away.

"Who are you, tiny human, to have entered my domain?" The voice boomed, forcing cold water against Nicholas's face.

He turned around to look for his friends, but could only see the alligator in the darkness.

"I'm Nicholas Blackwell."

The alligator rose, his head the size of a house. A red collar wrapped around his thick throat. A gold tag hung from the collar with the name *Khan* etched across it.

"The last living Blackwell, are you? How peculiar." The alligator shook his head. "Impossible. Blackwells are not tiny like you, but of average height."

"We used magic," Nicholas answered, as he coughed up muddy water, which made him gag.

"You know magic? Come now, dazzle me." The alligator's immense body plopped into the water, waves rippled against his scales. "Perhaps I will enjoy your incantations enough for me to spare your life. Doubtful though, I'm rather hungry."

"But I don't know any mag—" The way the alligator opened his mouth and raised his scaly brows made Nicholas stop. "What I meant to say was, I might know a few tricks." The alligator closed his mouth. "But you have to close your eyes."

"I will not close my eyes. I am smarter than the average 'gator. I guess you'll just have to suffice as a meal rather than my entertainment."

Just as the alligator opened his massive mouth, the serpent's head rose between them, out of the mucky water. Khan closed his mouth, bowing to the Great Serpent.

"My Lord, how great of you to visit me."

"*You know this boy to be a Blackwell, do you not?*"

Khan trembled, causing more waves to crash upon Nicholas. "I do, My Lord."

"*And still you hunger for him?*"

"I am sorry, My Lord."

The serpent lashed like a whip, wrapping its body around the alligator. Khan thrashed and squirmed, rolling through the water. The serpent's long, powerful body tightened around his throat, until the massive beast lay dead in the water. The serpent loosened its grip, head waving toward Nicholas bobbing in the water.

"*I killed my pet for you. This will be the only time I save your life. You're on your own from here on.*" The serpent dove into the water.

The water carried Nicholas down the sewer. He took the crystal sphere out from his pocket again and used it like a flashlight. All he could see was rushing water. He called out for Amy and Pugdush, but no one replied. Bats screeched, a couple came into view.

The current quickened, the roar of water up ahead growing louder. The light of the sphere revealed a drop. *A waterfall?*

Gripping tightly to the crystal sphere, Nicholas braced for the fall. His stomach knotted as he dropped, impossibly long, before plunging into the water below. He kicked up until his head broke through the surface. The current stopped, the river opening into a wide shallow pond. His feet were able to touch the bottom. He stood, looking up into the black starless sky above him. Strangely enough, despite the lack of stars, gray light illuminated the surroundings, like that on a gloomy day beneath a deeply overcast sky.

It looked like countryside. Pumpkins grew on either side of the pond, lined by a cornfield that looked to be unattended for years. A rundown shack loomed a few yards away.

A hand grabbed Nicholas by the arm and helped him out of the water. He looked up and was relieved to see Amy and Pugdush, dripping wet.

"How did you guys get here?" Nicholas asked.

"The same way you did. The water carried us," Amy said.

Pugdush pointed across the pumpkin yard to the rickety shack. On the porch was an old woman rocking back and forth on a wicker chair. Her withered face was infested with wrinkles. Crusty, villainous lips frowned toward them. Milk-white hair was chopped brutally into a pixie cut, scalp visible in patches.

"Who is she?" Nicholas asked.

"Her name is Socordia," Pugdush announced. "She is the Guardian of Sloth."

"The serpent led us here," Nicholas said.

"Why would the serpent point us in the right direction?" Amy asked.

Nicholas shrugged. "Not sure, but he seems to be helping me. He saved me from an alligator when we all got separated." He looked across the pumpkin yard to his next challenger. "Might as well get this one over with."

They heard a muffled screech, but couldn't place its source. It seemed to be coming from the dead thicket of cornstalk. Nicholas hesitated before pushing apart the tall weeds and forcing through.

Pinned up to a large wooden stake was a man wearing a long wool coat. A tall, pointy hat sat on his head. Nicholas's stomach knotted as he looked at the man's mouth. It was sewn shut by a thick cord of string. The man lifted his head and looked upon Nicholas with two black buttons for eyes. Nicholas slowly exhaled. This was not a man, he realized, but a scarecrow looking back at them. It seemed alive and aware, though, as it jerked toward them, producing another screech through his trapped mouth. Amy gasped.

Nicholas reached forward and pulled off the string, freeing the scarecrow's lips. Its body quivered.

"Thank you…"

"Shouldn't have done that," said Pugdush. "He is a human, punished for a horrible sin."

"No sin deserves such suffering." The scarecrow coughed up fluff when he spoke.

"What did you do?" Amy asked.

"Killed a bunch of people," he said. "Now, cut me down from here."

"Killed people?" Nicholas asked.

"It was nothing. When I was alive, I massacred many. But death caught up with me and I ended up here. I paid my dues. Now let me down! I can't suffer anymore. Please don't let me suffer," He whimpered, his face screwed as if crying, even though no tears came from the button eyes.

Nicholas took a step forward. "Why should you be spared suffering, when I'm sure you didn't show kindness to any of those you killed?"

The scarecrow ripped his hand free and grabbed Nicholas by the throat. His face pulled close to Nicholas. "We children must pay for the sins of our fathers. My father made me who I am. I am his shadow, the outcome of his cruelty. From the moment I was born my soul has been imprinted with the burden of his sins. He taught me to kill, to hurt and torture. I tried to stop the cycle, but death fueled my life. I needed it. I craved it." He tightened his grasp around Nicholas's throat. "Each child must pay for the sins of their father. So what will you endure, young sir? What will be your payment? That I wonder." He grinned toothlessly. Even though his eyes were buttons, they were still full of terror.

Pugdush smacked the scarecrow away. "Leave Nicholas alone!"

The three of them huddled close together, out of the scarecrows reach.

"Kill me. I beg of you." The scarecrow's eyes skipped from Nicholas to Amy to Pugdush.

"You're already dead," Amy said.

"Destroy my soul." With one hand, the scarecrow unbuttoned his shirt. There, in the middle of his chest, was a beating black heart, dripping with ink.

Nicholas shivered. The scarecrow's suffering seemed horrible. But to think that he tortured and killed others and apparently thought nothing of it…

"I don't think it's our place to decide your fate." Nicholas took Amy's hand and pulled away from the scarecrow.

The scarecrow screamed at the top of his lungs, "*Kill me!*" He repeated himself as though a knife was stabbing him over and over again.

Nicholas led the way through the pumpkin yard. He had never felt so tired in his entire life. Every muscle in his body ached. All he wanted was rest. He forced himself to continue walking. The scarecrow's screams faded, but they still filled his head.

Was it his place to decide a punishment for others? Was it his place to deny mercy, even to a despicable murderer? He didn't know what was right anymore, but he knew he would never be able to forget this scene.

The witch called Socordia eyed them peculiarly, as though she thought her trespassers to be a curious bunch. Her old, weathered hands gripped the arms of the wicker chair, as she rocked slowly back and forth.

They stopped a good distance away. Nicholas and Amy stood shoulder to shoulder. Pugdush stood in front of them, back leaning against Nicholas's knee.

"Hello, mumsy," Pugdush said.

She grinned. A wave of darkness swirled in her hand, materializing into a wand. About a foot in length, it looked like a thin carved stick with letters etched delicately across it. Her wrist moved in a circular motion as she spoke in a sharp voice, cutting like glass. "Corrupt servants of the magnificent dark, I beckon you with these words of my monarch. Arise from your sleeping graves, fulfill your purpose as my slaves." She raised her wand.

A silver spark flared overhead, smashing into the yard. A wave of silver splashed over the pumpkins, cutting through them, carving them with faces. Triangular eyes opened, newly-shaped mouths pouring out seeds until they were hollow.

Nicholas, Amy and Pugdush stepped back in fear as roots ripped out from beneath the pumpkins, rising to look like bodies underneath the grotesque pumpkin heads. Like a demented army, they gathered shoulder to shoulder, waiting for their mistress' request.

"Kill," Socordia uttered through pinched lips.

In unison, they advanced. Their haunting faces glared at Nicholas, Amy and Pugdush, as they chanted in rhythm with their march. "*Kill. Kill. Kill.*"

"What do we do now?" Nicholas asked.

"Socordia nothing without wand. Take wand, she too lazy with no magic," Pugdush said quietly.

Amy looked down at Pugdush, "So, that must be her piece of the Crown?"

Pugdush nodded.

*Kill, kill, kill.* The army of pumpkins surrounded them, tightening the circle with each step. Socordia flicked her wand and weapons materialized in each of the pumpkin men's hands. Swords flung in their direction. Nicholas pulled them down just in time to dodge the attack. Amy unhooked the dagger she had taken from Marluxia's slave and gripped it in her hand. She threw the blade at a nearby pumpkin man. Socordia's soldier fell over, and Nicholas snatched the pumpkin man's sword and began swinging through nearby pumpkins. Pugdush yanked the dagger out from the chest and tossed it back to Amy, who caught it like a professional.

"You be better with that than Pugdush," Pugdush said.

Nicholas held out his new sword, two hands wrapped around the handle. *Kill… kill… kill…* His blade slashed through the closest pumpkin. A spatter of entrails showered the yard. Nicholas smiled. Holding a sword gave him confidence. Again and again, his sword sliced, sending more pumpkins down.

Socordia cackled eerily from her rocking chair, as if amused with her entertainment. "There's something unusual about the girl. Bring her!" she ordered.

Roots in the shape of a hand gripped Amy's arm right above her elbow. The pumpkin man yanked her forward and she landed, skidding on her knees. She screamed as the pumpkin man dragged her through the dirt toward the witch.

"Let her go!" Nicholas yelled, two pumpkin men barring his way to saving Amy.

Pugdush ran under a pair of root legs and leapt up over a body. Using a pumpkin head as a spring, he launched himself at the pumpkin man dragging Amy. He knocked the head off, and the body fell to the dirt. A root hand still tightly clenched Amy's arm. As she ripped free, the headless body stood back up and seized Pugdush by the scruff of his neck. Pugdush pulled his tiny legs to his waist and pressed his arms to his chest, trembling. The pumpkin man expanded his roots to create a cage and tossed Pugdush inside. He reached for his pumpkin head, now missing a chunk out from the side, and placed it back on top of his body, then marched forward to Socordia.

"My own son," Socordia said to Pugdush. "A Risen demon? You sicken me. Defending the side of good." She spat.

"Pugdush sorry he disappoint mumsy."

"Punishment for such treachery will be found in the death of your new companions."

"No, please. Kill Pugdush. Not friends," Pugdush begged.

Socordia slammed a fist against the arm of her chair. All the pumpkin men collapsed at once. Nicholas and Amy stood in amazement.

"Friends? You care for these humans?" she demanded.

Pugdush slowly nodded his head.

She looked at him in disgust. "You will die as well." Her hand shot into the cage. Her old fingers wrapped around Pugdush's throat tightly. She yanked him out and brought him closer, dangling Pugdush in front of her face. "What is she?" Socordia pointed to Amy.

"Pugdush don't know. Pugdush just knows that Miss Amy is not like other humans."

Nicholas stepped in front of Amy, shielding her from Socordia. "Leave her out of this."

Socordia's wand slashed the air. A cut ran down Nicholas's cheek. He gasped, pressing his hand to his face, feeling blood seep through his fingers.

With all his might, Pugdush kicked the wand out of his mother's hand sending it across the yard.

Nicholas understood without words. He dove into the dirt and seized the wand with his blooded hand. At once, Socordia wailed in pain as she wilted into dust. The wand glowed as it sucked the dust into its base.

Nicholas zipped open his backpack and shoved the new piece of the Crown inside. Pugdush shook himself, clambering up to his feet.

Nicholas turned to Amy. "Is it true? You are not human?"

She averted her eyes.

"What are you?" he demanded.

 # THE CHAPEL OF DREAMS

Nicholas clutched his backpack as he paced through the pumpkin yard. Four Princes were defeated, and each of their pieces of the Crown was now in his possession. He also had the crystal sphere that housed a child's soul. He took out the sphere and held it in his palm, gazing into it as though he could see the boy's soul lingering beneath the surface.

"Pugdush know of a place where soul be safe."

Nicholas turned and knelt down so that their eyes were level. "The only place this soul will be safe is with me."

"You really think that is the smartest idea?" Amy chimed in. "We're in search of the Guardians of *Sin*. You think bringing an innocent soul for the ride will be in the boy's best interest?"

"What would you prefer me to do? Leave him in the woods?" Nicholas stood up. "Besides, what makes you think I can trust you? I don't even know what you are."

"That's absurd. I'm Amy."

"How do I know that?" Nicholas turned sharply to Pugdush. "And how did you manage to forget to mention that your mother is a Guardian of Sin? So, what does that make you, the heir to the Throne of Sloth?"

"No!" Pugdush folded his arms and pouted. "Mumsy had a litter of seven. I am the youngest. The one and only Risen of the bunch."

"Nicholas, you're being ridiculous," Amy said.

"Am I?"

Before Amy could respond, a stream of smoke swam past them. They turned in the direction the smoke was coming from, and saw Ramiro. Out of his shop, the demon looked odd. His back was swollen to the size of a pillow, his potbelly hung over his kneecaps, and his eyes were more droopy than usual. Ramiro leaned over a cart with his hookah resting on top, sucking smoke into his mouth, then belched white rings into the air.

"There is only one place safe for that boy's soul," Ramiro said.

Pugdush smiled. "Pugdush tried to tell them, Master Ramiro."

"How did you get here?" Nicholas asked.

"Never mind my means of travel. So much is at stake, and you two would rather argue. Foolish and irresponsible." He lifted his snout. "I come to assist you once again, though this time must be the last. Too many demons are disturbed by the fall of the four Princes. Sharp eyes are lurking now more than ever." Ramiro checked his surroundings for any disruption in the circling wilderness. "Now, there is a haven within the walls of Demonio. One sanctuary that binds the Good. A place where Evil can't go, no matter what. If hearts are pure and motives untainted, then refuge may be found in the Chapel of Dreams."

"The chapel of what?"

"Of dreams," Ramiro answered, dull teeth grinding with irritation. "In the chapel, a sanctuary is given to the Risen, though it will only show itself to those worthy of purity." Smoke dripped out of the corner of Ramiro's mouth. "The boy's soul will be safe there as you continue forward."

"How do we get to this Chapel of Dreams?" Amy asked.

"Pugdush knows." The little demon jumped up and down several times. "How does that rhyme go? Pugdush always forgets…" He scratched his forehead. "Oh yes:

> Imagine a place with all your wonder,
> Where evil foes can no longer plunder.
> Where kindness and loyalty are in the brave of heart,
> And ending wickedness is only the start.
> I swear my honesty and strip my malicious themes,
> And ask passage to the Chapel of Dreams."

Light poured out from the trees. In awe, Nicholas and Amy turned to it, their breath taken away. Then, the light slowly faded, leaving behind a tall chapel standing alone in a forest meadow. Sunlight shone through its stained glass windows, showering them in a rainbow of colors. Elm trees rose in a circle around it, scattering the meadow with golden leaves. The sunlight beamed down on the chapel, coating it in light, leaving the meadow in shade that deepened in the forest beyond.

They advanced, passing through a group of dead trees, stopping at the elm trees. Swarms of glittering fairies fluttered along the blooming flowers. A group of girls in long golden gowns danced hand in hand in a circle to the music they hummed.

Warmth radiated from the chapel embracing their bodies like a hug of sunlight.

"Welcome to the Chapel of Dreams," Ramiro said. "Now come, you must speak with Master Thril and Master Ling."

"Who?" Nicholas asked, unable to draw his eyes from the spectacular view.

"They are the founders of the Chapel of Dreams. The highest on the hierarchy of Risen demons," Ramiro answered. "We must hasten. Come forth."

Ramiro led the way toward the chapel, dragging his hookah cart through the rich field. The grass underfoot was soft, warm. The sweet scents of honey, water, and grass enfolded them. Amy closed her eyes for a moment, embracing the feeling. Pugdush sniffed, his face blissful. A sudden warmth wrapped Nicholas's hand, as though unseen fingers were entwined with his own, followed by a faint whisper he could have sworn was his mother's saying, *I love you, son.* Nicholas decided not to question the feeling, but instead enjoy the moment before it was gone.

The tall oak doors to the chapel opened before them, and a man in a cream apron stepped out. He wiped his hands clean and welcomed them with a smile.

"You four have been expected," he announced.

The sphere in Nicholas's hand cracked and then drifted away into a shower of silver dust. The dust collected, forming the little boy. He ran into the field and a group of children appeared in front of him, a large golden dog running around them.

"Come now. There is much to explain." The man led the way up a small flight of stairs. Nicholas helped Ramiro carry his hookah cart. Together, they entered the chapel.

The ceiling was high, the broad widows built with colorful stained glass. Walls were covered with frescoes and mosaics of angels and saints. Lanterns hung from the beams, dangling on thick chains. The pews were arranged toward a podium, which stood near a blazing pit of fire.

Many creatures filled the chapel, some resembling the stuff of nightmares, others not as frightening. Nicholas thought it odd as he watched the beasts bowing, praying, and pleading silently to the religious statues along the walls. He realized that unlike his usual trips to church, these creatures were not there because they had to be, but because they came of their own free will, hoping for a relationship with God.

"Master Thril and Master Ling knew you would come," the old man said.

Nicholas now noticed that the man was not human. His ears were long and pointy, his mouth frozen in a permanent snarl. An elf? Or a strange sort of demon? Everything seemed possible in this surreal world.

They followed their guide down the aisle to the end of the chapel. A strong odor of incense overwhelmed Nicholas. He stared.

On the podium stood a pig wearing a long robe and a pair of glasses. *Theodore.* He was preaching to a group of other pigs Nicholas recognized as servants to Prince Gullah. Nicholas wanted to say "hi", but his friend looked so happy he didn't want to disturb him.

They stopped at a single door at the very back of the church. The elf-man opened the door and led them through. They found themselves in a small room with stained glass windows stretching across the walls. All the designs were of angels and creatures that reminded Nicholas of fantasy novels he liked to read as a child. Lit candelabras cast a gentle glow throughout the room, creating a serene environment.

In the back of the room, laying on a mountain of ornamental pillows were two men, identical in appearance. Twins? Looking closer, Nicholas realized that they were. In fact, their bodies were not fully separate, united at the waist by a band of skin. The twins' mouths were molded like a toad's, tusks projected from under their lips. Bushy white eyebrows connected in the middle, and horns similar to a ram's twisted from their foreheads. The twins had cream-colored skin with faded brown spots and eyes as orange as the final rays of a sunset. Painted across the wall behind them was a beautiful woman with dark red curls and a chiseled face, painted beasts scattered around her.

"Greetings, Masters Thril and Ling," the elf guide said.

"Nicholas Blackwell," said Thril.

"Amy Glen," said Ling.

"How good it is to meet you both." Their voices sounded alike, as if they shared the same vocal cords. "Would you care for something to drink?"

"Please," Amy said. Nicholas's and Pugdush's expressions of gratitude followed hers. Ramiro only shook his head.

"Tea?" offered the elfish-man. He handed each of them a decorative glass, then pointed to the small wooden stools. They sat and sipped their tea, sweet, fragrant and refreshing like no tea Nicholas had ever tasted before.

"Thank you, Ramiro and Pugdush, for bringing them here. We had hoped to meet them," Thril said, before taking a sip of his own tea. Though his hands were as long and as strong as an ape's, Thril held his tea glass delicately between his thumb and index finger.

"Pugdush happy to do so, Master Thril."

Ramiro inhaled his smoke and puffed out a cloud. "No trouble at all, Your Greatnesses."

Ling studied both Nicholas and Amy. "Now, I understand that you two are in search of the Devil's Crown. Am I correct?"

"Yes," Amy answered. Nicholas nodded.

"I also am aware that Ramiro told you that the Crown can be held here for safe keeping," Ling said.

"After it helps take us back home," Nicholas added.

"Of course," Thril said. "Do you understand how grave the safety of the Devil's Crown is? Understanding its secrets will be quite crucial."

"Who exactly are you two?" Amy asked.

Thril frowned. "I thought you were already told. We are the founders of the Chapel of Dreams. Defenders of the Good, warriors of the Divine." He slurped his tea, surprisingly loud in the room's silence.

"Are you demons?" Amy asked.

"Yes and no," said Ling. "We are a part of the Risen. Demons that have stripped away their demonic ways, such as Pugdush and Ramiro here. We protect the Risen and help them along their journey of penance."

"What exactly is a Risen demon?" Nicholas asked. "Fallen angels are exiled from Heaven. They've fallen. But every Risen demon we've met is here, in Hell."

"First of all," Thril croaked. "It would be naive to mistake Demonio for Hell. I assure you the two are distinctly different."

Ling agreed with a slight nod of his head. "Tell me, how do you set apart good and evil?"

"Morals," Amy answered.

"Morals indeed," Ling agreed. "So would you not separate good and evil by birthright?"

"No."

"It's all about nature versus nurture," Thril added. "You see, Amy, we demons are born out of pure evil. To strip one's demonic ways is not something one can perform overnight. It is a lifelong commitment. There are rules and regulations. We must survive our punishments. Make right for what we have done wrong. Surpass our divine retribution. We Risen aren't just allowed to leave Demonio and enter the Mankind's World."

"Very few Risen demons have ever made it above ground," said Ling. "As you might have heard, demons are only allowed in the Mankind's World for a short period of time. The world opens to us only at 3 a.m. and closes at the first light of day."

"To become a true Risen would mean complete penance, to strip away all demonic ways," added Thril. "We here in the Chapel of Dreams are a part of an organization that stands for the Rise of the Phoenix."

"What do you mean by the Rise of the Phoenix?" Amy asked.

Thril leaned back in his seat. "What do you know of Demonio?"

"It is the city of demons. The resting place of the Guardians of Sin. The gateway to Hell," Nicholas said.

"True, yes, but understanding the history is just as important," Thril said.

Together, the twins pointed to the painting of the woman behind them. Thril leaned over and lifted a heavy book that had been positioned prominently against a nearby pillow. Drawn on the thick leather cover was a unicorn, crafted by a most skillful hand. The title, engraved in golden letters underneath, read, *Fabula: The Origin of Secrets.*

Thril put on a pair of glasses and began skimming through the crisp, old pages. Once he found the story he was searching for, he began, "Some believe her story is what you might call a fairy tale. An ancient myth, collective folklore, or perhaps a skeptical fable. Whatever the description, the story begins thus: eons ago, when the Mankind's World was new, humans were created. Living among them were creatures of magical influence, known as the Enchanted. They were not created by God. The Queen of the Enchanted was a phoenix who had the power to take on human form. Her name was Inanna, the first Enchanted to be born into the Mankind's World."

"Inanna was the Enchanted's version of Eve," Ling added.

Thril glanced at him sideways, as if displeased at the interruption, then cleared his throat and continued, "A myth relates to her connection to the fall of the first angel, Lucifer, God's most gifted angel." He lifted his bushy eyebrows. "It is a common fact that Lucifer was defiant against the Lord and disgraced the Divine, but what history has kept concealed was that Lucifer was in love with Inanna. They kept it hidden as long as possible, but in the end it did not make a difference. An angel was not to love another the way Lucifer loved Inanna.

An angel's love is meant to spread over many, similar to the way God loves all of his children. Lucifer and Inanna entwined themselves in forbidden love."

"So, what happened?" Nicholas asked, intrigued.

"As you know, Lucifer became the first fallen angel. Cast away. Exiled from Heaven."

"Because he was in love?!"

"Because of his betrayal. His twisted love was only the beginning. You see, Lucifer was the most beautiful of all God's angels. Even the archangels didn't compare to him. Vanity overcame him, fashioning the first sin: *pride*. He thought that if he was so gifted, then why wasn't he God himself? He wished for his throne to be above the stars of the Lord. Higher than any cloud. So, he was cast from Heaven, bringing with him one third of God's angels."

"I thought angels were good?" Nicholas asked.

"Just like man, angels were created with a free will," Ling said.

"Free will," smirked Thril. "As some might say, the one flaw in the grand design."

"We are what we choose to be, young Blackwell," Ling said. "Nothing more, nothing less. That means evil can be found in any heart, even an angel's."

"What happened next?" Nicholas prompted.

"Inanna and Lucifer were very powerful. To protect themselves from each other, they exchanged sacred gifts." Thril pulled out from behind him what seemed like a hefty piece of metal; a shield with ruby jewels in the shape of a phoenix. "When Lucifer and Inanna committed themselves to one another, Inanna forged this shield. It is said to be the only thing impenetrable to the glorious fire of the Phoenix." He handed the shield to Nicholas. It was oddly light, no more than the weight of a feather. As he touched it, the shield glowed and shrank into an amulet the size of Nicholas's palm.

"Whenever you wish for the shield, use this amulet to call it forth and it will appear to you."

"You mean I can keep it?" Nicholas couldn't believe his eyes.

"Until you complete your quest. You'll need it."

"Thank you." Nicholas closed his hand over the amulet.

"But what do the Devil's Crown and the Guardians have to do with Lucifer or Inanna?" Amy asked.

"The Crown belongs to Lucifer," Ling said.

Thril continued, "In return for the Phoenix's shield, Lucifer gave his Crown to Inanna. While Inanna wore the Crown, Lucifer would not be able to harm her. The Crown was designed to wield powers unknown to anyone but Lucifer. It is rumored that one of its many privileges is to make a Risen demon permanently Risen."

"And then…?" Nicholas asked.

"War," Thril answered. "An epic battle that engulfed the Mankind's World was fought between the angels. Animals united themselves with the angels, and the Enchanted stood beside their Queen and allied with the fallen angels. The Enchanted became the vessels of demonic souls. Thus, came the birth of demons.

"Now, Lucifer was pleased with the war. His pride would not break. But Inanna had seen the suffering of her Enchanted. She pitied them as she witnessed their souls darkening by magic. She felt as though she had disgraced hundreds of her subjects because of her forbidden love for Lucifer. So, she wrapped herself in fire and trapped Lucifer in a lake of her inferno."

"Which created Hell," Ling added.

Thril nodded. "She sacrificed herself, and thus ended the war. However, the story was never finished, and a myth was born. Some believe she gave birth to Lucifer's son. To protect him, she built a magical city for her Enchanted. She thought that once her son was old enough, he would be their ruler and lead Inanna's people into the Golden Age. But as an infant, the child's innocence was vulnerable to Lucifer's corruption. So, she hid him deep in the city and appointed her most trusted followers to be his Guardians and look after her baby.

"To strengthen these Guardians in case Lucifer sought out his son, Inanna broke Lucifer's Crown, separating it into seven pieces. She gave a piece to each Guardian, giving them strength over the Devil himself. But Lucifer was manipulative. He tempted each Guardian with their deepest, darkest desire. In return for learning the child's whereabouts and gaining safe passage to him, Lucifer would allow them to keep their piece of the Crown, and he would give them power over their own desire—one of the seven deadly sins."

"What happened to the boy?" Nicholas asked.

"No one knows the truth," Ling answered. "Some believe Lucifer killed him in revenge for Inanna's betrayal. Others believe he took the child in and made the boy the final Prince of Hell. The strongest of them all. The Guardian of Pride."

Thril leaned forward. "But the real legend begins with this: the Rise of the Phoenix. It is said that the Phoenix will be reborn from her ashes, and she will bring the final war between Good and Evil. Some believe she will be evil, others believe she will defend the Good. We all wait for her to be reborn from her ashes.

"We, Risen demons, represent the Phoenix. We put our faith in believing that Inanna will return, that she will rise from her ashes and defend us like she once had. We believe she will wear the Devil's Crown and restore us permanently, purifying our wicked souls. However, other demons believe Inanna will return evil and lead the final war into darkness. Regardless of which side Inanna chooses to stand for, her moral stature will determine the outcome of the final war. It is said that no blood from either angel or demon will have to be spilled, because the Phoenix's chosen faith will be the victor. Her faith alone will be the new world order."

"How do you know the story is not just a myth?" Nicholas asked.

Ling smiled. "Every myth stems from truth, young Blackwell."

"So, what now?"

"Four pieces of the Devil's Crown are at hand. Go back into Demonio, and search for the last three Guardians." Thril looked directly at Nicholas. "But beware the Great Serpent. He tests you." His voice trembled.

Nicholas opened his mouth to tell Thril and Ling that the Serpent had saved him on more than one occasion, not to mention pointing him in the right direction to Socordia. But Thril's fearful expression stopped him.

"Alright," he said instead. "Where's the next Guardian?"

"Head back to the streets of Demonio. Somewhere there you will find what you seek," Thril answered.

Nicholas, Amy and Pugdush gathered in the doorway.

"What will happen to that little boy's soul?" Nicholas asked.

"We'll send him home to his family," Ling answered.

"And Theodore? He's still a pig."

Thril chuckled, "Your friend Theodore has been a great contribution to our Chapel. Once you've brought the Devil's Crown to us, we'll send him home along with you two. As a human."

"Thank you," Nicholas said.

"Farewell. Take heed of the darkness," Thril warned.

"Follow your hearts," Ling suggested. He studied Nicholas's face. "See not with your eyes my friend, but with your mind. Witnessing the world this way might unravel secrets you might not have ever expected. He who can imagine can discover the impossible."

On that note, Nicholas, Amy and Pugdush left the Chapel of Dreams. The little boy waved his goodbye from amidst his laughing playmates. He looked happy. Nicholas felt warm as he waved back before following his friends into the wilderness.

Whatever happened to him, knowing that he saved this boy made all the dangers they faced seem worthwhile.

# THE YELLOW BRICK HOUSE

They found themselves back in the pumpkin yard. Trying not to look at the broken pumpkins scattered everywhere, at the wicker chair standing beside the empty hut, Nicholas turned into the woods. Cold fear seized his heart. Glowing yellow eyes lit up in the darkness between the trees, following Nicholas and his friends with their unblinking stares. The path was bordered by leafless trees, the ceiling of branches arching overhead. They were silent as they walked, the faint sound of owl hoots, cawing of crows, and strange inhuman groans echoing in the distance.

Suddenly, a mighty sparrow swooped overhead. They turned as it landed on a tree branch. Its fierce claws gripped the wood, wings folding against its feathery body. Nicholas stared.

The sparrow's face was human, but with a curved beak in place of a mouth. Frizzy hair stood in thick cords, wavering around its head. Its face was shadow-dark.

"Come, children," it screeched sharply. "Follow me."

With a flap of his wings, the bird soared overhead. Nicholas, Amy and Pugdush took off after it, jogging through the forest. The bird glided across, wind gusting through its feathers.

"Why are we following that thing?" Amy asked.

"Who knows?" Nicholas said. "We don't have many choices."

"Pugdush never seen such beast as that," Pugdush said, rubbing his hands together nervously. "Frightening enough to bring fear to demons."

The bird-like demon led them into a clearing. A house built of sunshine-yellow bricks stood in the middle, bordered by a white picket fence. The bird swooped down, landing on the edge of the chimney.

"Oh my God," Amy uttered in disbelief.

"What is a house like that doing in Demonio?" Nicholas wondered out loud.

"Pugdush don't like the look of this. Something so pretty in such a dark world can only mean trickery," Pugdush warned.

Amy fixed her eyes on the structure before her. She kept on walking, and Nicholas followed, through the white gate into the garden beyond. Flower scents filled the air. The bird-demon perched on the rooftop ahead of them. Its wing feathers fused together to create a cloak. His claws fell away, his limbs extending as he made his way across the roof, the feathers melting away to revealing the milky-white skin, colorless hair falling onto his shoulders, yellow wings behind his back…

"The Demon of Destiny," Amy gasped.

Nicholas stared, remembering one of the two twin demons they met in a forest clearing playing chess.

The demon perched on the edge of the roof, beckoning. "Come, little ones. See the past before you as though it was the present. Just remember: you mustn't be recognized or time will twist."

With a wave of his hand, the door to the house blew open and Amy rushed toward it.

"Amy, wait!" Nicholas rushed up the steps after her, Pugdush hurried to keep up.

They stepped into a large room, their steps echoing over the polished hardwood floor. A cream-colored couch stood to one side, along with the mahogany furniture. A cozy fireplace crackled with fire, floral wallpaper adorned the walls.

"What is this place?" Nicholas asked, he and Pugdush coming up behind Amy. He wondered why Amy looked so entranced, as if she had seen a ghost. There seemed to be nothing threatening in this fairly ordinary room. He walked to the brick fireplace. A fire crackled inside, pleasantly warm after the chill outside. A series of pictures spread across the mantel. Nicholas eyed the closest one, a little girl with overpowering red hair. He picked the picture up and looked back at Amy, noticing the uncanny resemblance of the two.

"Put down that picture!" snapped a woman, from the kitchen doorway. She hurried through the living room, walking through Amy as if she was a ghost. Nicholas opened his mouth in surprise.

The woman snatched the picture from Nicholas's grasp. Her hands trembled as she wiped the glass with her shirt and placed the picture reverently back onto the mantel.

"How did you two get in here?" She looked Nicholas and Pugdush up and down.

"The door was unlocked," Nicholas answered.

"So, you make a habit of coming into homes with unlocked doors?"

"Pugdush sorry."

"You had better be." She pressed her hands together and sat down on the couch. Nicholas realized she was trembling. *Is she afraid of us?*

"What are you doing here in the middle of the forest?" Nicholas asked. He glanced at Amy, watching the woman from the corner of the room, her back pressed against the wall as though she needed something to support her.

The woman raised an eyebrow. "Forest? We are in the middle of London."

"London?"

Pugdush tugged on Nicholas's sleeve. "Pugdush think we might be stuck in time warp."

"What do you mean?" Nicholas asked.

"Not only demons live in Demonio. Sometimes souls from the Mankind's World come here when they commit a great sin. Like the scarecrow."

"What are you two rambling on about?" the woman snapped. "It's rude to talk about someone as if they're not there. Especially in their own home."

"Pugdush sorry again."

Nicholas snatched the picture back from the mantle. "Who is this girl?"

"Please. Don't. My baby." She covered her face with her hands. Amy looked the other way, tears sliding down her face.

"What is your name?" Nicholas asked slowly.

The woman pulled her red curls behind her ear. "Annette Glen. Please, give me back my picture."

Nicholas looked back to Amy, her face was buried in her hands as she sunk to the floor, knees pulled up to her chest. He handed the picture back to Annette. "By any chance, is your daughter's name Amy?"

"Yes." She stroked the picture. "My little girl. I'll see her again." She heaved a breath. "I know I will."

"What happened to Miss Amy?" Pugdush asked.

"She ran away." Annette reached into her pocket and pulled out a bottle of pills. She wiped her sweaty brow and then gulped three pills down. "Why…?" She looked back at Nicholas, who didn't know how to respond. "She was so beautiful. Dark red curls, fair skin, evergreen eyes, she could dazzle anyone. I wish I'd never fought with her."

"What happened?" Nicholas asked.

"You're sweet to care." The woman smiled sadly. "I remember that day better than any other. She'll come home again. One day. She'll come home like nothing ever happened." Again she tossed a handful of pills into her mouth, chewing on them as if they were candy.

"I don't think you should be taking so many pills," Nicholas said.

"My pills are the only thing that make the pain go away."

"Mama, I'm here!" Amy exclaimed.

The woman didn't respond, as if Amy wasn't there.

"What happened to Amy?" Nicholas prompted.

"It was January 31, 1955."

"1955?" Nicholas raised his eyebrows. He glanced at Amy, but she avoided eye contact.

Annette continued, "Amy had just come home from a ballet concert. She had talent scouts who'd come from colleges across America watching her, wanting her to come to their academy. She was so talented, she could have done anything she wanted."

"And then?" Nicholas asked.

The woman curved her lips. "Burnett Ellsworth, his name was. He promised her instant fame. You see, Amy knew she couldn't go to college because we had no money. Mr. Ellsworth seemed like the gentlemanly sort. She believed him. And I…" She turned away, her lips trembling.

"You… what?"

The woman shook her head. "I had too much to drink that night. I fell asleep. The next morning, the police officers woke me up. They said…" She covered her face with her hands, dissolving into sobs.

Nicholas stepped forward and placed a comforting hand on her shoulder.

"They found her…" the woman cried. "In the park… My baby girl…. her neck snapped, her face bruised… her body twisted…"

Nicholas turned to Amy. Her lips trembled.

Annette looked up to Nicholas as she popped a few more pills into her mouth. "Please leave now." Her eyelids became heavy. "I need my rest."

Amy stepped toward Annette and wrapped her arms around her mother, tears dripping down her face. "I'm so sorry, mama. I'm so sorry." Her body trembled as she touched Annette. Annette's lips tugged into a slight smile. Her body leaned into the couch, eyes closing.

"Is she dead?" Nicholas worried.

Amy's lips quivered as she nodded.

"We stuck in time warp," Pugdush said again.

"What exactly is a time warp?" Nicholas asked, staring at the dead body in front of him.

"Good and Evil made a treaty long ago. Souls would go to Heaven as long as they avoided the three unspeakable crimes: bigotry, murder, and suicide."

"Bigotry?"

"Hatred for no reason. God created the Mankind's World in hopes we love each other as brothers. Bigotry is hatred toward those who are different—by race, ethnicity, gender, sexual orientation, religion… Bigotry is hatred at its finest, the exact opposite of love. It's not just hatred, but acting on hatred."

"So, what about the time warp?" Nicholas asked.

"Souls that commit suicide without being forgiven by God will be trapped in a time warp and will continue to repeat their crimes for eternity. No matter what we could have done, the outcome will forever be the same. Annette is a lost soul. Which means we are close to the Gates of Hell."

Amy buried her face into her hands. "I have to go."

"Amy wait," Nicholas called, but Amy ignored him and ran into the hallway.

She reached the restroom and forced the door open. Nicholas followed her. Amy looked like she knew her way—of course she would. After all, she grew up here. 1955? Murdered in a park? Nicholas still couldn't make sense of it. He stopped in the doorway and saw Amy enter.

The restroom was in disarray, a shower curtain torn, the wooden floorboards damp and moldy. The rusty faucet sat over the cracked counters. Amy twisted the tap. After a moment, black water gushed out, slowly turning clear. Amy cupped her hands together and splashed the water onto her face, then brushed her hair back, pulling red locks behind her ears. She was so upset she didn't see Nicholas watching. Suddenly the door slammed shut and separated them.

"*Amy Glen,*" an icy voice whispered. "*What would you give to save your mother from her current prison? What would you sacrifice to save her soul? She killed herself, because of you. Because of you, her soul has been condemned to continue suffering. Because of you.*"

Nicholas leaned toward the keyhole and saw the head of the serpent rising out of the toilet, its blue eyes glaring at her. Like a train shooting through a tunnel, its body emerged, coiling onto the floor. It rose up tall, head just below the ceiling.

"*What will it cost, Amy Glen, for you to leave Nicholas Blackwell? Depart from Demonio and go back home. Forget your mission and never look back.*"

Amy trembled. "Never."

"*I am not after you. The boy is what I desire. Stand in my way and you will suffer like your mother.*"

"What's going on?" Nicholas yelled, throwing himself at the door to burst it open.

The serpent's head whipped around. Its lips lifted into a twisted smile. "*The final war rages near. All protection will be forgotten. Your blood will be expendable, girl. Just ask Gabriel.*"

"Gabriel? What did you do to him?" Amy demanded.

The Great Serpent's grin looked smug. "*A Prince of Hell has captured him. The Guardian of Wrath now tortures him. The final battle draws near. Choose your side wisely.*" The serpent slithered back into the toilet bowl, water splashing over the floor.

"What just happened?" Nicholas asked.

Amy looked back to Nicholas. "We have to find the Guardian of Wrath. Quickly."

Just then, a little red-haired girl ran past her. She turned and beckoned before disappearing down the hall.

 DARK DESIRE

Nicholas and Amy rushed after the girl, leaving Pugdush in the living room to watch over Annette's body. The little Risen demon was not happy, but once he found a glass bowl of tiny chocolate squares, he quickly agreed.

Nicholas trailed Amy up a flight of stairs at the back of the house. On the second floor, the same flowery wallpaper covered the walls. Doors opened on each side, but Amy ignored them all as she followed the girl to the end of the hall. The girl tapped the knob and laughed, then disappeared.

Amy seized the doorknob and twisted. The door creaked open.

Nicholas stepped after her into the petite room, glancing around with curiosity. The vanity stood by the far wall, the metal-framed bed beside it covered with a violet comforter. A tall oak bookcase leaned opposite it. The room looked old, abandoned, yet he could still sense Amy's presence here. 1955. How was this all possible?

Amy slowly made her way across the room and stopped in front of the bookcase. Her hand swept across the middle shelf, fingers tracing every book, a perfume bottle, stuffed toys. She stopped at a small green box, clutching it tightly as she held it up with a look of shock and bewilderment. She flipped the top of the box open and a ballerina rose up, twirling to the gentle hum of a lullaby. The melody drifted out, soft and angelic. Amy joined in with the song, piecing the words together as though remembering a distant memory. Suddenly, her body wilted away and swirled into the box without warning. For a moment the music box floated in mid-air.

Before Nicholas could scream, a set of crippled hands materialized, supporting the box. Thin, bony arms followed, and then an emaciated torso, covered in a white shroud.

The male form continued to reveal itself like a disease, spreading down and up. Next came a pair of thin, buckling legs paired with bare feet that pointed slightly inward. Last came the head: a face of true terror. His skin was blue, as though it was frozen in water, with dark purple circles around his eyes. Long, shaggy hair fell down his blistered face. His head cocked toward Nicholas with an expression of curiosity.

"You're next," he rasped, beckoning Nicholas closer.

Nicholas froze. "Wh—what did you do to Amy?"

"Hush."

Nicholas felt his body wilting away. It was an odd feeling of losing substance, twirling, spinning as he was pulled inside the box. The demon scrapped the box with his yellow fingernail.

"Go on, my friends, show me your hearts. Reveal to me your inner hopes. Your haunting dreams are my dark desires."

Amy lifted her leg to the railing along the wall of the dance studio. Her foot bent, toes straightened. Her tights hugged her body, giving her movements freedom. She gracefully raised her hand over her head and leaned into her body, causing her muscles to stretch further. She caught a glimpse of her reflection in the mirrors that made up the walls of the small room. Her body tingled with excitement. Her dreams of performing were finally coming true.

"Amy."

She whirled around on her toes. There was her mother, in a beautiful gown, shimmering earrings and a sparkling diamond necklace. Her face showed pure happiness as she smiled at Amy. "Are you ready, sweetheart? It's almost time."

Nicholas woke up in a well-lit room. He quickly rose and rubbed his eyes. For a moment, he couldn't remember where he was, then the familiar details settled in, one by one. A large room that seemed enormous after seeing Amy's tiny bedroom. Flat screen television fixed on the wall, with video games stacked beside it in a tower. The desk in the corner, housing a massive computer monitor. He looked down at himself. He was wearing silk pajamas, with his initials embroidered on the chest.

Nicholas's heart raced as he hurried out of his room and looked down the polished wood banister to the first floor. Oliver Blackwell sat on a recliner, flipping through the channels on the television. Nicholas hurried down the stairs, skipping as many as he could.

The house was just how he remembered it: luxurious furniture, glossy wooden floorboards, modern artwork decorating the walls. A Christmas tree, adorned with lavish ornaments, that seemed right out of a holiday film, stood facing the window overlooking the street.

"Hey, sleepyhead," Oliver said. "Come watch the game with your old man."

Nicholas finally noticed that though the man seemed to be his father, Oliver's face was only a blur. Nicholas stepped back. Why couldn't he remember what his father looked like?

"He doesn't have time to watch the game," said Kathleen Blackwell, emerging from the kitchen with a tray of freshly baked cookies. Her face was also a blur like Oliver's. "Nicholas, it's almost time for Christmas dinner. Don't you want to get out of your pajamas?" She laughed softly.

"Yeah, but first can you tell me what happened to your faces?"

Oliver and Kathleen shared a glance.

"Whatever do you mean, dear?" Kathleen said warmly.

"You alright, champ?" Oliver asked.

"I guess so."

Kathleen took Nicholas by the hand. "Come on, there are so many people I want you to meet. They're all joining us for dinner."

Oliver stood up and took his other hand, ushering Nicholas through the doorway into a regal dining room with a table large enough to seat at least twenty. Around the table stood a crowd of people. As they noticed Nicholas entering, they broke into a round of applause.

"Nicholas Blackwell!" some cried out. Flashes from cameras caught Nicholas by surprise.

"Who are they?" Nicholas asked.

"Your fans," his mother answered.

"Nicholas!" shouted a woman that looked like a news reporter with a tape recorder in her outstretched hand. Three video cameras pointed toward him from different angles and a dozen cameras constantly flashed, capturing Nicholas's image. "Tell me, Nicholas Blackwell, how did you defeat the seven Guardians of Sin?"

"I don't remember," he answered.

Oliver laughed, "How modest my boy is. A true Champion of Sin."

Kathleen hushed the crowd. "Everyone, please take a seat. Dinner will be served in just a few moments. I'm sure, after dessert, Nicholas would love to share his story." She leaned into Nicholas. "Would you do me a favor and get Isabella out of bed?"

"Who's Isabella?"

Kathleen just laughed as if her son had told the most hilarious joke she had ever heard. Nicholas decided not to ask again, but to go upstairs instead and search for the mysterious Isabella. Everything seemed so bizarre. His parents had no faces, news reporters wanted to know how he defeated the Guardians of Sin, and he was told to wake up a girl he had never heard of. Not to mention his dead parents were actually alive and hosting a dinner party. His mind felt hazy, as though his memories had suddenly shattered and the pieces were left misplaced. Though dream-like, it still felt good. He had a family again, his parents who loved him and wanted to celebrate the holidays with him. More than that, reporters were itching to tell his life story.

Nicholas hurried up the staircase, looking around his New York City home he hadn't seen in nine years. The house looked the same as he remembered, even the lemon scent of furniture polish was familiar. Nicholas walked down the hall and stopped at the bedroom door beside his own room. His hand wrapped around the doorknob, not knowing why he chose to stop at that particular door. He pushed it open and walked into the nursery.

A crib stood in the middle of the room. Two oversized stuffed animals sat beside the crib, a unicorn and a lion. Nicholas approached the crib and peeked inside. A tiny baby girl with black hair and dark blue eyes stared back at him. *A sister. I have a sister… I always wanted one.*

"Go on, Nicholas," came a raspy demon's voice. "Tell me your desire. What do you wish for more than anything in the world? Perhaps a family is what lingers in your innermost hopes. Or this could be a distant memory. Unravel your family's dark secrets."

Annette took Amy's hand and they hurried through the studio. They stopped at the edge of a dark stage. Black curtains pulled open to reveal a cheering audience. Annette embraced Amy in a tight hug.

"Good luck," she whispered. "You'll do great. The talent scouts are going to be in the first row. They're all waiting for you."

"What about you?"

"I'm going to be right here. I want the best seat. Now, go, do what you were born to do." Annette gently pushed Amy onto the stage and instantly it illuminated with spotlights. The audience became silent. Amy focused and settled her nerves. She glanced back at her mom, unseen by anyone but her. Annette nodded her head solemnly.

Amy lifted to her toes and dramatic music started. Her body twirled, her legs kicked, feet extended, her movements perfect like a dream as she gracefully glided across the stage to the music. In the middle of the act, a male dancer appeared on stage. Amy leapt into his arms. He spun then lifted her, showcasing her to the audience. As he brought her back down and they faced, she realized that it was Nicholas. He lowered Amy to the floor. She stepped back gracefully, and Nicholas took her hand and twirled her, then pulled her toward him. She forgot the dance as their bodies leaned into each other, lips barely apart.

"Go on, Amy," taunted the demon. "What do you choose, to perform for millions or to protect the man you desire? What will you give up to save his soul?"

The music came to an end. Nicholas's face became fuzzy, morphing into a man Amy did not recognize. Her heart raced. None of this was real. But Nicholas... She jumped off the stage and raced down the aisle toward the exit.

As she forced the door open and leapt through, she found herself in a ballroom. The floor was lined with marble, and dozens of men and women, all dressed in elegant suits and gowns, danced hand-in-hand. Amy dove into the crowd, shouldering through the dancers.

"Nicholas!" she shouted, hoping he was here.

Nicholas looked down, his eyes meeting Isabella's. His head pounded as if fighting through an endless, mind-boggling riddle. *What does it mean? What does any of this mean? What was this demon trying to show me that I didn't understand?* Then it struck him like lightning. *What happened to Amy?* He turned away from the infant and left the room.

Instead of the familiar hallway he found himself in a ballroom, in the center of the dance floor. Couples danced around him, gliding across the marble floor.

"Nicholas!" Amy shouted.

Nicholas turned around, and there she was, pushing past a dancing couple, straight into his arms.

She raised her eyes to him, frowning. "I was looking for you, but I thought... I don't even know what I thought. This place is so confusing."

"No kidding. I saw my parents, but they had no faces. Then, I saw a baby girl named Isabella. Where were you?"

"Dancing."

"Really?"

"No, not just dancing, but performing... It used to be an unfulfilled dream of mine."

"Having my parents and a family used to be my dream," Nicholas said. "What does it mean?"

"We both said *used to be*." Amy paused. "In this dream just now, why did you leave your family behind?"

"I was looking for you."

"And I was looking for you."

In the middle of the dance floor the demon appeared. His frail body slunk between dancers. His blue face twisted in a grim smile. "Dark desire," he rasped. "Leave this purgatory for a price. Give up your dreams. Amy, you will never dance again. You, Nicholas, shall never know your sister, Isabella. I will keep your dreams and distant memories. Give them to me and you may leave, unharmed."

"Nicholas? Miss Amy?" Pugdush cautiously walked up the staircase to the upper level of the cottage, chocolate smeared across his fuzzy face. He walked straight along the hallway, to the end where he opened the bedroom door.

The demon lay across Amy's bed, eyes closed, chest expanding slowly. Pugdush poked the demon, but he did not wake. He climbed up the mattress and reached for the music box clutched in the demon's hand. The top opened and a small, plastic version of Nicholas and Amy lifted and twirled in place.

Pugdush frowned. "Demon of Dark Desire. Let Pugdush friends go!" He slapped the demon's face, but still the demon did not wake. Pugdush pried the music box out from the demon's fingers and jumped off the bed. "Nicholas! Miss Amy!" Pugdush shouted into the box. "Don't give the demon your dreams! If you do, you will return as zombies. Dreams are our souls, you can't give them away or you will never be the same. Wake up!"

"Did you hear that?" Nicholas looked at Amy.

Amy nodded. "Pugdush."

Nicholas took Amy's hand. He pulled her into his arms. His lips leaned into her ear. "Trust me. I know what I'm doing." He turned to the demon and nodded.

The demon smiled, then snapped his fingers and the ballroom melted away. It felt to Nicholas as if being kicked in the stomach, his mind whirling violently as the dancers spun in circles faster and faster around them. Then they too faded and they found themselves in Amy's bedroom. The Demon of Dark Desire was nowhere to be seen, the music box lying forgotten on the bed.

Pugdush cheered. Amy looked at Nicholas.

"How did you know that we wouldn't be affected by giving away our dreams?"

"You said it yourself. What we say used to be our dreams. Not anymore. I think I have a new one." He lifted a half smile toward Amy.

She smiled back.

"You lucky," Pugdush said. "Demon of Dark Desire powerful. Dream you gave up will come back to haunt you both."

# THE ELDERS
# OF FEAR

Before they left Amy's house, Nicholas had draped a sheet over Annette's dead body. Shortly after, the body disappeared and Annette was back in the kitchen as if nothing had happened, crying over the loss of her child.

"Who are you?" Annette spotted Nicholas and Pugdush in the living room.

Nicholas couldn't collect the energy to answer. Instead he turned to the door and followed Amy out onto the porch. He put a hand on her shoulder. She closed her eyes and fell into his arms, face buried in his chest, eyes stung by tears.

"It's okay, Amy. I'm here for you."

Pugdush cleared his throat, "Pugdush, too."

Nicholas lifted her chin and looked into her eyes. "Amy, I want you to know I'm not going to ask you about what Annette said. Whatever you're hiding from me, I trust you have your reasons."

A moment of silence seized the porch. Only now Nicholas noted that snow had begun falling while they were inside. The forest around them was blanketed in white.

Suddenly, a demon wearing a long black cloak popped out of a cluster of thorns. Yellow-white wings escaped through the slits of the cloth at his back, flapping, but flightless.

Nicholas recognized the Demon of Death, whose twin, Destiny, had led them into Amy's house.

The demon's pale face contorted with rage as he waved a trembling finger. "You were supposed to die in there! I wrapped you up like a gift for the Great Serpent and yet he spares you...? It is not in his nature, as it is not in mine, to allow your souls to leave that home in their human vessels."

"We didn't die in there, so you cannot have us," Amy said.

"They were never meant to die there." The Demon of Destiny appeared out of nowhere, standing between Death and Nicholas. "They were there to learn something. To advance their own destiny."

"They should have perished!" Death roared. "I claimed their souls. I won the chess match. Not you. They are mine. I own them!"

"Their souls are too important to be wagered in a chess match," Destiny said.

"You say that because you lost."

"They must fulfill their *destiny* before you claim them," Destiny pointed out.

"I want them now." Death stomped his foot into the snow. "We will speak to the Councilmen."

"As you wish, Death. Come, children." Destiny beckoned them.

"Like Hell we're going with you!" Nicholas said.

Pugdush tugged Nicholas's hand. "Cannot disobey Destiny or Death. If they wish for you, you have no choice but obey."

"We only have three more Guardians to fight. There's no way we're going."

"Very well," Destiny said. He clapped his hands toward Nicholas and Amy. Instantly, their bodies shrunk and changed. Amy had morphed into a white rabbit with long floppy ears and

Nicholas had changed into an Alaskan malamute puppy with the same dark, blue eyes.

Pugdush knelt down and looked into the puppy's face. "Nicholas?"

The dog barked in response.

"Pugdush be back for you." Pugdush took off into the woods, running as fast as his tiny feet would allow.

Death turned to run after the small demon, but Destiny blocked his path. "Pugdush is no concern of ours. You may claim him later, as promised."

Death agreed, and together they walked up to the porch. Death clutched the rabbit by her ears and Destiny seized the dog. Then they vanished.

The two demons reappeared back in the city of Demonio, in the middle of a string of broken-down buildings. A black stone tower stood in front of them. Thunder crashed, followed by the zigzag of lightning that flashed in the night sky. They came to a swinging door and pushed through, entering a lobby with a chipped, marble floor. The ceiling was far above them at the top of the tower. They stood in the middle of the lobby with a mosaic beneath their feet depicting a malicious unicorn. Death cleared his throat and the carving of the unicorn lifted onto a platform.

"Password," spoke the unicorn, its voice harsh like the screech of metal chains. "If death is the beginning, then what is the ending?"

Destiny cleared his throat, "Death has no beginning, nor ending. Life is certain."

Death rolled his eyes.

"Close enough," the unicorn announced. The platform shot up, rising fast to the ceiling, then came to an abrupt halt at the top of the tower.

It was a dark room. Silver engravings of demons along the walls gave off faint illumination that didn't penetrate the shadows of the ceiling. Five podiums stood tall in its center, each with a silver plate on its side spelling a name. Two of the middle ones were empty, higher than the rest. The other three were occupied by demons. One had no face, just a black hole for a mouth. His silver plate spelled "Disease". His neighbor had a skeleton face adorned with shreds of dripping skin, "Famine." The third, with a monstrous jaw larger than his face, mouth filled with razor sharp teeth, had "Hate" written on his podium. Horns on his forehead sat like a crown, twisting in odd directions.

Destiny and Death left the rabbit and dog on the unicorn platform and climbed up to their podiums. Once they were comfortable, Destiny clapped and Nicholas and Amy morphed back into their human forms.

"What just happened?" Nicholas asked. He could not remember anything past Annette's home. He huddled close to Amy, watching the demons.

"What is the meaning of this, Death and Destiny?" the Demon of Famine spoke.

"Two souls equally between the grasp of Death and myself," Destiny answered. "They must be judged by the Council and sentenced appropriately."

"Exciting," groaned the Demon of Disease.

"Release us," Nicholas demanded.

"You have no authority here, Nicholas Blackwell," Death informed him.

"He is a Blackwell?" Disease asked.

"Certainly," Destiny said.

"Tasty," the Demon of Hate added, licking his lips. He pulled down his jaw and stuck his massive tongue out from his mouth, as if tasting their scent.

The Demon of Famine grabbed his eye and tugged it out of its socket. He stretched out his hand, so that his eye could look closer upon Nicholas and Amy. "Excuse me—my eyesight isn't what it used to be. I see the resemblance of the Blackwell men." He dangled his eye further down by its optic nerve, like a child with a yo-yo.

"Who are you, demons?" Nicholas asked.

The Demon of Famine coughed. He scratched crust off the corner of his mouth and then began, "We five make up the Archdemons of Terror. The Elders of Fear."

"Archdemons? Never heard of you."

"Have you not heard of Famine? Or Disease? Perhaps you've heard of Hate? Death? Destiny?"

"Well, yes, but—"

"Then, you've heard of us," Famine said. "Our standing among our fellow demons is very high. We are above all demons, just below the seven Princes, respectively."

"We defeated four Princes. Would that mean we're stronger than you five?" Nicholas asked.

The Demon of Hate cackled. "You have yet to see how strong we are. All of our powers reach the Mankind's World without us leaving this tower. You want to see how it works?"

"No, thanks," Nicholas ran his fingers through his hair.

"Back to the issue at hand," said the Demon of Destiny. "Who claims their souls?"

"If he is truly a Blackwell, we shouldn't touch him," Disease spoke.

"It all depends on his moral standing," added the Demon of Death.

"Obviously." Famine smirked. He leaned over his podium, leering at Nicholas. "What are you boy, good or evil?"

"Good," Nicholas answered, surprised at the certainty he felt.

"I'm afraid that won't be tolerated." Famine sat back in his chair, shaking his head.

"What is that one?" the Demon of Hate pointed a hairy finger at Amy. "She looks delicious."

"I see light. Blinding. Disgusting," snarled Disease.

"I know what she is," Destiny said. "But for some reason she wishes to keep it a secret from the boy."

Nicholas glanced back at Amy. What was she hiding? Why wouldn't she tell him?

"A secret?" Famine cocked his head. "Well, now I'm getting hungry."

"This is my case," announced Destiny. "These two souls are much too significant to lose just yet. I wish to see their outcome. Point them in the right direction."

"My case," announced Death, "is to kill these two travelers. Claim their souls for our own. We have already lost four of our Princes. Do we really want to risk losing more? End this madness now. Kill them both!"

"The Guardians of Sin must be tested constantly," Disease said. "Their power weakens if not challenged. It is the cost of becoming a Guardian. They do not just represent Demonio, but Hell and all of the demonkind. If they continue to fall, then perhaps they are undeserving of their piece of the Devil's Crown. Perhaps new Princes should be nominated to take their place."

"Let's not forget that the boy is a Blackwell and is more than capable of dethroning a Prince," added the Demon of Hate.

"Then what to do with them?" asked Disease.

"The Great Serpent wishes to test the two, or he would never have allowed passage to Demonio," Destiny reminded.

"Or just maybe the Great Serpent wishes to test his Princes," said Famine. "Remember, the final war is on the horizon. The Guardians of Sin are our greatest warriors. Should they fail a Blackwell, they won't stand a chance against an army of angels."

"Kill them," Hate rasped.

"We must vote first," Disease interjected. "All in favor of allowing passage through Demonio, raise a hand. Or a claw. Whatever it may be."

The Demons of Famine, Disease and Destiny raised their hands.

"It is decided. You may go forth and challenge our Princes," Famine said.

"But it doesn't mean you'll survive," Death grunted. "I'll be back for you." He locked eyes with Nicholas one final time before the unicorn platform shot down. Nicholas's stomach felt like it was still in the top of the tower by the time the platform landed back in the lobby. The two of them staggered off and made their way to the swinging doors.

"Where to now?" Nicholas asked, as they stepped back into the street. His head was still spinning from the fall through the tower.

"We need to find the Guardian of Wrath," Amy answered.

Suddenly, a roar echoed through the street, bouncing off the walls. They turned to see a blast of flames shoot into the black sky.

# THE BOILER ROOM

Flames shot up into the sky. Street lamps and building lights flickered on and off with each blast of fire. Demons cluttered the street, watching in awe.

"What's going on?" Nicholas asked.

Amy shrugged.

A nearby goblin, its pig-like body complete with a corkscrew tail, looked at them, his head turning a complete circle like an owl's. "Pyro must be angry." He grinned menacingly.

"Is that the Guardian of Wrath?" Nicholas asked.

"Sure is." The goblin pointed across the city to a cluster of tall buildings. "Just beyond those buildings, on the edge of Demonio, lies his lair. The Boiler Room. I wouldn't pay him a visit though."

"Let's get going," Nicholas said.

He took Amy's hand and they hurried through Demonio, shouldering through crowds of demons. They followed the blasts of fire flaring across the sky past the cluster of buildings, standing on the edge of a gorge. At the bottom, a metallic warehouse rose out of a rumble of rocks, much wider than it was tall, its roof cluttered with pipes that belched black smoke into the murky sky.

A rickety wooden ladder at the edge of the cliff descended into the gorge. Nicholas went down first to test it out. Once he reached the bottom, Amy followed. The ground was hot, warmth soaking through their shoes. As they continued on toward the warehouse, Nicholas could feel anger rising through him. It felt overpowering, like acid destroying his insides, corrupting his emotions and twisting his thoughts to morbid fascinations. He clenched his fists, fighting the urge to start swinging at the closest thing.

"*Help us,*" whispered a faint voice.

"*Mercy. I beg of you, mercy,*" another said weakly.

"*Nicholas Blackwell,*" a group of voices said as one. "*Mercy Nicholas, mercy on us. Save our souls from wrath.*"

"Can you hear those voices?" Nicholas turned to Amy as they stopped at a tall, broad door, the entrance to the warehouse.

"What voices?"

"Never mind." Nicholas curled his hand into a fist and knocked.

There was no answer. For a good while, they stood waiting, then stepped back and peeked around the warehouse for another way in. Just then, a burst of fire blasted from inside the warehouse and threw the front door wide open, narrowly missing them.

From within the flames came a cruel, harsh voice, "Who dares come to my Realm of Fury?"

Nicholas stepped forward. "I, Nicholas Blackwell, challenge you, Guardian of Wrath, Prince of Hell."

"Blackwell. I heard of your fighting against four of my brothers across Demonio. Come, if you dare."

The flames stopped. Nicholas looked to Amy. With a nod of "okay," they entered the warehouse.

A red carpet stretched across the room. Human-sized cages lined the walls, one after another, with torches in between.

Each housed a prisoner. As Nicholas and Amy made their way past, imploring hands shot out from between the bars trying to grab at them.

"*Help me, Nicholas. Save me from wrath.*"

"*Nicholas.*"

"*Nicholas, I know Amy's secret,*" enticed a wicked voice. "*I know what she is. Unbind my chains, liberate my soul from this merciless existence and I will divulge her cryptic tale.*"

"*I know a more compelling secret,*" offered another cruel voice. "*The Blackwell family secret.*"

Taunting voices overlapped each other, sending chills down his spine.

"Shut up!" Nicholas shouted, hands pressed against his head trying with all his might to suppress his boiling anger.

"Ignore them." Amy gripped Nicholas's hand.

"I thought you said you couldn't hear them."

"I lied," she admitted.

Nicholas looked into the closest barred cage. Framed against the blackness was a thin man, his raw skin ripped in many places, muscles and bones visible from each fresh cut. His fingernails dripped with blood. His upper lip tugged into the most wicked smile Nicholas had ever seen, displaying black gums and chipped teeth.

"What are they?" Nicholas thought of reaching for his inhaler, but decided against it as he calmed his anxiety with deep breaths.

"Pained souls trapped in agony," Amy answered. "Kind of like my mother. But she is stuck in her personal sorrow. These prisoners are stuck in their twisted, dark reality."

"*Horrible agony, Nicholas. Great pain haunts me. It tears me to shreds,*" the nearby prisoner spoke, trembling hands holding ripped pieces of his skin. He slipped into the shadows, leaving only darkness in the cage.

The voices were weighing down on Nicholas's chest. Starting from the front door torches began dimming. Slowly, they went out one by one.

"*Don't let the lights go out,*" screeched a prisoner. "*Terrible things happen in the dark. The Great Serpent may only return through the shadows of the heart.*"

They came to the end of the room. Nicholas turned a doorknob and forced the door open. In the chamber ahead, a maze of machinery was making strange noises, coughing out clouds of scorching hot steam. They slowly made their way across the chamber, avoiding the steam. Tiny gremlins, two inches tall, scurried across the pipes that ran along the ceiling, pulling out wires and plugging them into different outlets. Two more were jumping up and down on a pipe, bending it. One gremlin, fatter than the others, twisted a knob. Steam blasted out from a nearby pipe sending the fat gremlin flying across the room.

The next room they found looked more like a massive cave. A thin bridge made from what looked like clusters of coals extended across the room to a hill, where a beast as large as two elephants sat. A red-horned dragon craned its neck, its massive face waving toward Nicholas and Amy. Spikes hung from the ceiling right above the dragon's head. A birdcage, tall enough to house a man, dangled beside it. In the cage stood the janitor of St. Christopher's Academy.

"*Gabriel?*" Nicholas squinted his eyes toward his janitor's cut-up face.

"Oh, no," Amy muttered.

"We have to rescue him," Nicholas said.

"Nicholas Blackwell," roared the dragon, wind gusting out of his mouth, almost knocking Nicholas and Amy over. "I am Prince Pyro, Guardian of Wrath. I accept your challenge." He spread his spiked wings.

Nicholas gaped. Was the dragon going to fight him? There was no way he could win this by combat.

"What's the virtue that counters Wrath?" Nicholas said, voice trembling.

"Patience."

He gulped.

The dragon flapped his wings, lifting his immense body up into the air. Nicholas's heart raced. Could there be a weakness in the dragon's underbelly? He looked closer and smiled. He found his target.

Pyro soared toward them, blowing a blast of fire onto the coal bridge, setting it aglow. They jumped back from the heated coals. The dragon landed on the bridge, chunks of coal crumbling at his touch; falling pieces showered down into the pit of darkness below. Mesmerized, Nicholas and Amy watched the glowing coals fade, consumed by the dark depths.

"Won't you fight?" asked Pyro. "You challenged me, therefore you must give me a challenge. Your insignificant life is too easily won."

"Why are you so angry?" Nicholas asked.

The dragon laughed, steam shooting out his flaring nostrils. His mouth boiled with fire. "Unlike my defeated brothers, I have overcome my virtue. Patience will not weaken me." The dragon stood up on his hind legs, as tall as a tower. Nicholas noticed a golden sword sticking out from the thick scales that shielded his chest. Pyro stomped the ground, tremors knocking Nicholas and Amy over.

"I'll distract him," Nicholas whispered to Amy. "You make a run for Gabriel." He reached into his backpack and pulled out the ruby amulet, holding it up until it stretched into the shield. The ruby gems that made up the phoenix glowed brightly. The heat receded. *Does the shield make me immune to fire?* Nicholas reached toward the coals scattered on the floor, amazed at how he could now touch them without burning his hand. He grabbed a handful and ran forward, throwing pieces of coal at the dragon's face, aiming for his golden eyes. Out of the corner of his eye he could see Amy sprinting across the burning bridge. He continued throwing the coals against the dragon, angering him more and distracting him from Amy.

Pyro's jaw lunged forward, jagged teeth the size of swords snapping toward Nicholas. He dodged the attack and threw another coal, this time hitting the eye. Pyro roared in pain, neck craning, scales pulsating like gills.

Amy climbed the hill at the end of the bridge where the dragon had slept. Her hands gripped the bars of the oversized birdcage.

"Amy, you must finish your task and take Nicholas out of Demonio." Gabriel sounded weak. She barely recognized him, cuts and bruises masking the beauty of his face. His right eye was badly swollen.

"We're almost finished, Gabriel. We only have three more Guardians left!"

"We have risked too much in allowing Nicholas to come here." Gabriel's hands grabbed Amy's through the bars. His ghostly white face looked haunted and sick. "I was wrong, Amy. The Blackwell family secret is nothing like I had ever expected."

Amy turned to Nicholas, enticing Pyro by throwing coals while still managing to dodge his attacks, though Pyro's snapping mouth was coming closer each time. She looked back at Gabriel. His face was pasty, hair stuck to his sweaty forehead.

"What secret?" Amy asked, looking into Gabriel's panicked eyes.

A jet of crimson flames shot overhead. Amy ducked and Gabriel fell to the floor of the cage to avoid getting burnt.

They both stood up. Amy looked at Nicholas again, fighting the dragon with his shield. Swinging it wide, he smacked Pyro's snout. The dragon's tail swooped around, aiming for his chest, sending Nicholas hurling backwards. He got to his feet, breathing shallowly, painfully, as he hurried back to Pyro.

"What do we do, Gabriel?" Amy asked, unable to look away from the fight.

"The risks involved are far worse than what we expected. These secrets are wrapped within history, going back eons, to the time when merlins existed."

"Merlin? Like the wizard?" Amy asked.

"Merlin was never a single person, but a title of a person who could predict the future."

"Gabriel, I don't understand. Are you talking about a prophecy?"

"There have only been a handful of merlins to have ever existed throughout ancient times. But the most powerful, renowned merlin, was at her prime during the missing years of the Bible."

"What missing years?" Amy asked, she felt like her mind was completely boggled.

"The eighteen missing years of Christ. Between the ages of twelve to thirty. During this time, a merlin by the name of Wysandra the Wise foretold an extraordinarily accurate prophecy. One that spoke of Armageddon. This foretelling predicted the final war between Good and Evil, and all that was to be expected. She wrote her prophecy into a poem, naming specific moments that would culminate in a great war that could engulf the Mankind's World. Shortly after it was written, the poem was lost. No one knew what Wysandra had written, until now. I followed you and Nicholas into Demonio, reaching Ramiro's book shop shortly after you two had left for Marluxia's mansion. There, hidden in Ramiro's library, was Wysandra's prophecy."

An inferno blast engulfed the bridge. Pyro flapped his mighty wings and landed on the hill. Amy hid behind Gabriel's cage.

Nicholas edged to the center of the bridge.

"What are you waiting for?" he taunted the dragon. "I thought you were a Prince of Hell. Not some cowardly, overgrown lizard!"

Pyro threw his head back, fire belching, blasting against the ceiling. A shower of flames shot across the cavern. Nicholas blocked the fire with his shield like an umbrella and Amy dodged each blast. The dragon roared, more fire blasting out from his mouth. Nicholas blocked the attack once again. He swung the shield into the flames and they ricocheted back, slamming into Pyro, sending him crashing against the bridge. Nicholas ran toward him.

Amy tugged at the bars of the cage trying to set Gabriel free.

"It's no use, Amy. The dragon knows master spells. These bars are enchanted. Unbreakable," Gabriel said.

Amy's eyes swept across the cavern to the backpack covered in burnt patches slung over Nicholas's shoulder. "Unless broken by magic," she smiled. "Nicholas, the wand!"

Nicholas jabbed Pyro in the jaw with his shield. The dragon roared, his neck whipping back.

"I need the wand!" she yelled, her voice echoing to Nicholas. He hurried across the bridge, a rush of coals collapsed after he had passed, thinning the bridge. Flames smacked the path in front of him. A portion of the coal bridge sheared away, leaving a gaping hole between Nicholas and Amy. With all of his might he lunged, jumping off the edge. His hands grabbed the ledge, shield slipping out of his fingers and spiraling through the darkness.

Amy ran to Nicholas and pulled him up as the dragon soared above them. They hurried out of the way as the dragon dropped to the hill, cracking the ground. He huffed, smoke shooting out of his nostrils. Great flames of fire emerged from the dragon's mouth. The golden sword in his heart glistened. Nicholas ran forward and grabbed the sword handle. With force, he pulled the sword out from the thick scales. He used the blade to slice a small cut in his own hand, then wrapped it around the sword handle.

The dragon roared in agonizing pain, claws pressed against his heart as he backed off the hill and fell through the darkness. A stream of ash rose up and was sucked into the sword.

Amy took the backpack off Nicholas's shoulder and unzipped it. She reached for the wand and sliced the air toward Gabriel's cage. The cage door sprung open.

Nicholas drew his inhaler out of his pocket and puffed into his mouth as Amy helped Gabriel. She turned, pointing the wand at the demolished coal bridge. She waved it gently and coals began to collect, gathering together, reforming the bridge. Her fingers cramped and a jolt of pain shot up her arm from the magic, leaving her hands covered in scabs. Trying to ignore the pain, Amy placed the wand back in Nicholas's backpack. She hoped she would never have to use magic again.

"You guys," Nicholas said, still out of breath. He was kneeling on the ground, hand wrapped around his side where blood soaked through his school uniform shirt.

"Nicholas!" Amy grabbed Nicholas's shoulder. "What do we do?" She glanced at Gabriel.

The young man stepped forward and moved Amy gently aside. Kneeling, he pressed his hand against Nicholas's heart. A wave of light washed across Nicholas's chest, dropped to his stomach and settled at his wound. Gabriel kept still for a moment, then rose and stepped away.

Nicholas lifted his shirt and felt his healed skin. His eyes widened as he looked at Gabriel. "Who are you?"

"Gabriel, an archangel of Heaven," the young man said.

"Oh my God," Nicholas said. "This whole time?"

Gabriel laughed. "Well, I didn't just become the famous angel overnight."

"You couldn't have told me before?" Nicholas swayed as Amy helped him to his feet.

"Would you have believed me?"

"I guess not." Nicholas smiled, cocking his head toward his school's janitor. "Where are your wings then?"

"Do you remember what Master Ling told you at the Chapel of Dreams?" Amy asked.

"He said a lot."

"Before we left, he told you to see with your mind, not your eyes."

Nicholas turned to Gabriel. *What the heck was that supposed to mean? See with your mind?* He stared, struggling to enfold it all. St. Christopher's janitor was the archangel Gabriel. No matter how hard he tried, he found it impossible to believe. But then again, how much had he seen since Demonio that he never before thought possible?

Then the sensation hit him like a tidal wave. Excitement crawled up his skin. It was sort of like Christmas morning for a child, when you knew Santa Clause had just left presents. The wonder overwhelmed him. And then he saw the wings. Tall, majestic, pristine white, silky feathers rising and falling in time with Gabriel's breathing.

As he watched, Gabriel's cuts and bruises wilted away. He looked beautiful. How could it be that Nicholas had never seen him for what he was before?

"Whoa," Nicholas gasped.

Gabriel put a hand on Nicholas's shoulder. "When you truly believe in something, your heart and soul will bring you that sight." He ripped off his blood-soaked janitor shirt and tossed the shreds aside. His torso was immaculate, sculpted like a perfect statue.

Gabriel took Nicholas by his shoulder. "Secrets were kept for good reasons, Nicholas. A series of cruel events started to follow you the moment you were conceived. Evil is after you. Demons killed your mother and your father and they wish to tamper with your innocence, corrupting your morals and darkening your faith. Two more Guardians await. Contain them in the Devil's Crown and end this madness. We are on the brink of the apocalypse."

"But we already defeated five of seven Princes," Nicholas protested. "They couldn't reach the Mankind's World even if they wanted to. They're gone."

"Nicholas, you may have contained their vessels, but their souls still exist. Each is contained within their piece of the Devil's Crown, but they can easily escape if the Crown fell into the wrong hands."

"The Risen demons want us to bring the Crown to the Chapel of Dreams for safety. Is that a good idea?" Amy asked Gabriel.

Gabriel shook his head. "I believe that the Risen demons want the Devil's Crown not for safekeeping, but because it will help them to complete their journey to the Divine. This is a selfish reason. We have much safer refuges for the Devil's Crown than the Chapel of Dreams."

"What should we do with the Crown once we're done with the Guardians then?" Nicholas asked.

"I want you to bring the Crown to me. Then we will find another way to bring you two back home."

"Come with us then. Help us defeat the Princes," Nicholas said.

Gabriel shook his head. "I'm afraid, Nicholas, that all my gifts are limited here in Demonio, where the Princes' powers are immense. Besides, I am needed at St. Christopher's Academy. In my absence, the school becomes penetrable by evil."

"Why would demons want to go to St. Christopher Academy?" Nicholas asked.

Gabriel smiled. "St. Christopher's Academy has its own secrets."

"Of course." *Great. More secrets.* He looked at Gabriel suspiciously. "How did you get to Demonio?"

"Through the Tunnel of Light."

"Can we get out that way?" Nicholas asked.

Amy and Gabriel shared a smile that made Nicholas feel his question was stupid.

"If you die, yes. The Tunnel of Light only gives passage to souls and angels," Gabriel said. "I'm sorry Nicholas, but in my attempt to rescue you two I've learned nothing that would help you get home. I wish I could have done more, instead of getting trapped and needing rescue. But I'll find a way, once you complete your task. I promise." He smiled. "I wanted to put an end to your journey. Pull you from this fight against sin. I had been so worried about you both since this all began. And now I see how much the two of you have grown. Together, you've accomplished great things. It was wrong of me to doubt. I now understand that I shouldn't interfere but keep my faith in you two."

Nicholas and Amy looked to each other. It wasn't until Gabriel's acknowledgment that they truly understood what they had accomplished together.

"I must go, but take this first." Gabriel knelt down and picked up the sword Nicholas had pulled from Pyro's heart. He handed it to Nicholas by its hilt. "It is my brother's sword, unbreakable. Stronger than anything man-made. It has been a very long time since this sword has been in the hands of Good. It was stolen, and is now one of the pieces of the Devil's Crown." As he spoke, the mighty golden blade retracted into the handle.

"Gabriel," Amy said, "what about the secret you were going to tell me?"

"What secret?" Nicholas asked.

"Perhaps, Amy, the secret is also best concealed from you as well. All you two need is each other's support." Gabriel turned from them. "Careful, you two." With a running start, he jumped off the edge of the hill. His wings expanded regally. He soared through the cavern, wind blowing through his feathers. Then a bright light pierced the ceiling and swallowed him.

# THE BLACK PEARL

Nicholas and Amy stood outside of the Boiler Room, unsure of where to begin their search for the last two Guardians. Nicholas leaned against the wall, mind racing with the images of Gabriel soaring across the cavern. How could he have not known who Gabriel was this whole time?

They both kept silent on their way back to the streets of Demonio. Dark clouds pulled across the sky. Rain showered the city, falling harder than Nicholas had ever experienced. The rain made walking difficult. They took cover beneath a rafter alongside a closed shop. Thunder boomed violently above, loud like a stampede of wild beasts. Rivers of water swept down the streets.

"Where should we go?" Amy yelled over the clatter of thunder.

Nicholas shrugged. He looked further down the street, where the edge of Demonio ran into a cluster of tall mountains. A palace stood there, one that neither Nicholas nor Amy had noticed before. Carved into the side of the hill, the mighty structure seemed to be a part of it, as if growing naturally out of the earth. He pointed, and Amy nodded, following him down the drenched street.

The palace seemed even larger as they approached. Nicholas couldn't believe they missed it before. Perhaps the palace revealed itself only now when he learned to see with his mind's eye?

As they neared, he saw the huge statue of a phoenix carved in white marble above the entrance. Its wings created a bowl where fire crackled, unaffected by the hard rainfall.

Nicholas advanced, his feet pounding through the deep rainwater as he hurried through the street. Amy quickly followed. They stopped at the entrance, their clothes drenched, their faces dripping with water. The marble phoenix loomed above him. Across the door tall gold letters read: *Blackwell Manor.*

Nicholas stared. "Why does that say my last name?"

"I have no idea," Amy said.

The water along the street rose fast, spinning in whirlpools as it flowed. A few small goblins got caught in the current and screamed as they were carried out of sight or swallowed into the whirlpools. Nicholas and Amy grabbed onto a street lamp for support as the water churned faster and stronger. It rose, until Nicholas couldn't hold on any longer. His grip loosened. Amy grabbed his wrist, her other hand holding the street lamp tightly.

"Hold on!" Amy cried.

"I can't."

A mighty wave rolled toward them, crashing between the buildings. The water hit them hard, ripping them apart. Nicholas flipped through the water, his back scraping against a stone as he washed into the whirlpool. Around he went, the current too strong to break free. Then he found that the current no longer held him. He swam, kicking as fast as he could. His head broke the surface.

He was no longer in the streets of Demonio, but swimming in what appeared to be a lake with black water. A cave opened in the distance, carved into a mountain, the only landform in eyesight. He scanned the area quickly, screaming for Amy, but his search only brought the three small goblins that had been sucked into the whirlpool before him. Their short, stubby arms desperately thrashed about as they tried to swim, but the water ultimately got the best of them.

Nicholas dove, searching for Amy underwater, but it was too dark and turbid to see anything. He emerged, looking at the cave. Although he was a trained swimmer, the cave was further away than it seemed and he had little energy left as he started toward it. Fortunately, a slight current seemed to be pulling him on, making his progress faster than he expected. Soon, he drifted in through the mouth of the cave. The scent of the salty water wafted through the air. Torches with green embers hung from the algae-infested walls, casting an eerie glow across the cavern. On an island, in the middle of the cave, stood a huge opened shell. A woman sat inside, as dignified as one might be when seated on a throne. Her ice-blonde hair flowed down her narrow shoulders, covering her breasts. A long scaly tail covered by cuts, new and old, started at her waistline, ending with a wide fin where the feet should be. She smacked it on the wet, glossy floor as she sat, her delicate hands wrapped around a black pearl the size of her fist. She looked at it with longing, peering into its depths.

"It would have taken you years to discover where I lurk, Nicholas Blackwell. I thought I'd save you the trouble and call for you instead."

Nicholas was surprised that she spoke to him. He thought the mermaid hadn't seen him, considering she had not once taken her eyes off the pearl in her hands.

Now that he was close enough to the island, he could see that the small piece of land was cluttered with statues, all of them female, some of full bodies, others of only broken-off legs.

"I know what you're after, Nicholas Blackwell," the mermaid said. "And I don't care." Her gaze finally shifted to Nicholas, and he could see the sorrow radiating from her eyes.

He shivered. Her eyelids were crusted with dried blood, black like sloppily layered eye shadow.

"What is that?" While studying the pearl, Nicholas tried to grip the island for a better look, but a sharp coral surrounding the edge cut his hands. He shrank back, blood oozing into the water.

"I've lived with this curse for much too long. I can't bear it any longer. I want legs." Her voice trembled, eyes soaked with tears, "*Human* legs."

"Let me guess, Envy?" Nicholas said.

"My brothers were easily taken because the sins that haunt them are seductive. Lust, Gluttony, Greed, Sloth, Wrath, they are all the fulfillment of their own desire. But envy is not a fulfillment, it's the continuous longing." Her eyes glistened. She rubbed her hands against the black pearl, body quivering, thin shoulders collapsing. Her outstretched hand offered the pearl to Nicholas. "Take my piece of the Crown, but for a trade. Your legs, for this."

"I can't just cut off my legs." Nicholas protested.

"I know enchantments." She flipped her hair over her shoulders. "It won't hurt. Please, just one spell and we can make the switch. I want to dance. I need to dance." Her other hand reached for a green music box beside her tail. She twisted a small knob several times and the top pulled up revealing a ballerina twirling in place. She hummed the melody as it played.

Nicholas stared, wondering how the mermaid had obtained Amy's music box.

Once the song ended, the mermaid snapped the box closed. "Can't you see? I want to be just like her. Why can't I be like her? Tell me!" She threw the music box at Nicholas. He ducked as it splashed beside him. "I apologize for my anger, it fuels me to madness."

"You're the first demon I have met who apologized for anything. Are you a Risen demon?" Nicholas asked.

The mermaid laughed, "I have caused innocents more pain in my life than most. No matter how *good* I could become, my soul is tattered beyond repair."

"What's your name?" Nicholas asked. He wasn't sure why he suddenly felt kindness for the mermaid. Perhaps he was starting to feel her sorrow?

"Vidia."

"Vidia, I feel your pain, your envy, but I need your help. Please help me."

"I need help, too. I need legs!"

"You have to compromise, Vidia. If I give you my legs, I won't be able to challenge the last Guardian. You know, envy used to tear at my insides most of my life. I watched my parents get murdered in front of me when I was seven years old. Growing up, I had no mom or dad to comfort me during a thunderstorm, or check under my bed when I was sure something scary was hiding there. I haven't had someone tell me they loved me in nine years. I envied the kids at school as they were dropped off by their parents. I hated them for it. I wanted my mom and my dad, but I couldn't have them. I know your pain."

"How does it feel to look upon your torturer? We Guardians influence our power throughout the Mankind's World, preying on the weak. My envy is what caused your pain."

"Hand me over your piece of the Crown and we can call it even."

Her face softened. "The last Guardian you will face must be fought differently than all the others. The last Guardian of Sin will be your greatest threat." Her eyes fell sadly back to her black pearl for a moment, then shifted to Nicholas. "I'm too tired to envy any longer." She tossed Nicholas the pearl.

He caught it with his uninjured hand and held it above the blood-muddled water. As soon as the pearl touched his blood, the sin of envy would be contained within its piece of the Crown. He hesitated.

"What are you waiting for?" Vidia's lips trembled. "Contain me! Contain me, Nicholas Blackwell. End this cruel suffering."

"I want you to know that out of all the sins I have fought, you're the hardest to contain, when you should be the easiest."

"Thank you, Nicholas. You are much more of a man than any I have encountered." Her eyes met Nicholas's and in that moment he could feel her soul. Wicked as it might be, it wasn't frightening, but hollow. She nodded her head, her body still trembling.

Nicholas lowered the black pearl into the water.

Vidia's body erupted into a shower of mist. Unlike the other Guardians, she did not scream. A sigh echoed through the air as a gust of wind blew toward Nicholas, mist soaking into the black pearl.

The water began to rise. Noticing the exit of the cavern disappearing in the rising water, Nicholas quickly stowed the pearl into his backpack and started swimming back. The water rose faster until his head touched the ceiling and the entrance completely submerged underwater. Seaweed wrapped around him, tying his arms. He closed his eyes. His stomach felt like it had just been kicked. A force thrust him up, out from the water. *The Great Serpent.*

He flew through the air and landed in a bed of rich grass in the middle of a beautiful garden. He lay, coughing up water. The serpent rose above him, head swaying toward Nicholas. It smirked, its long, scaly body snapping, bending in a hundred different places. Scales showered to the grass, the serpent morphing in front of his eyes, transforming into a handsome man. His serpent's blue eyes leered at Nicholas.

The man snapped his fingers and Amy appeared beside him, tied in a rope of smoke.

"Nicholas, run!" she cried, but Nicholas could not move as he stared back into the man's piercing eyes.

"Nicholas Blackwell," the man spoke in a rich voice. He smiled, cocking his head toward Nicholas, kneeling over him. "You have no idea what you have started." He stood back up, tall and regal. A dagger made of the same type of smoke as that binding Amy formed in his hand.

With all his might, the man stabbed Amy in the side. The blade ripped through the back of her shirt, freeing two beautiful wings.

Nicholas's mouth fell open.

Amy kept his gaze as she mouthed, *I'm sorry*.

The man whipped back around, gripping Amy by the throat. "If you wish to save her, you will find me." He disappeared in a cloud of black mist, taking Amy with him, leaving Nicholas gasping for air in the middle of a beautiful garden.

With a gasp, he recognized the garden in the middle of the woods where the Serpent had led him before.

The Garden of Eden.

 BLACKWELL MANOR

After a puff from his inhaler, Nicholas headed across the woods. If he wasn't quick enough, Amy was in jeopardy.

Finally Nicholas came across a familiar road leading back to the Academy. He looked both ways and darted to his right, across the asphalt. He was out of breath, probably should have used his inhaler again, but the fear of losing Amy kept him going. Soon, he spotted a tall iron gate. The two gargoyles along the top began to shriek like weak lions. He ignored them as he blasted through. The school never had seemed so far from the front gates as it did now.

Wheezing, he entered the building.

"Nicholas?" Dean rushed up to him, his arm wrapped around Becky's shoulders. "Where have you been?"

Nicholas only waved as he hurried across the hall. He skidded to a stop at the janitor's room, swung the door open, and fell in.

"What's wrong?" Gabriel dropped a mop into a bucket of hot, soapy water.

"Amy… angel…stabbed… Great Serpent… really a man… kidnapped Amy," Nicholas fought to catch his breath.

Gabriel grabbed Nicholas by the shoulder. "You did well, Nicholas. But now I need you to stay within the school grounds.

I have to go speak with the members of the Vatican. This is much more than I had ever anticipated. Go to Father Henry. Do not leave his side. Understand?"

Nicholas nodded.

Gabriel vanished into a luminous cloud of mist.

"I wish people would stop doing that!" Nicholas ran back out of the room. Despite his wheezing, he charged up a staircase to the second floor and ran past Sister Agatha and Sister Nancy. They both shot him bloodcurdling looks.

"Slow down," bellowed Sister Agatha, her turkey gobble of a neck flapping as she yelled.

"Sorry!" Nicholas called back.

He skidded, stopping at his most feared room in school. The principal's office. He stepped through the doorway, shivering as he looked at the fountain depicting the lion and the unicorn in combat. The unicorn reminded him of the bizarre demons in Demonio.

Father Henry lifted his head from his mound of paperwork. He took off his glasses and folded them, setting them down on his desk and staring expectantly at Nicholas.

"What could you possibly have done now?"

"Oh, just the usual: visited Demonio, the city of demons, challenged six of the seven Princes of Hell, contained them all. Got attacked by countless creatures. Found out that my school's janitor is actually an archangel, watched my friend sprout wings and get kidnapped by a snake who turned into a man. Nothing out of the ordinary."

Silence filled the room for a few long moments.

"Do you speak the truth?"

"Oh, no, just coming up with some fresh ideas for the school's winter play." Nicholas sighed in exasperation.

Father Henry lifted his eyebrow.

"Of course, I'm serious!" Nicholas shouted. "Gabriel went to go speak to the Vatican. He asked me to stay with you until he got back."

"So, he risks St. Christopher's Academy's safety by leaving school grounds?" Father Henry shook his head. "Too long have you been our burden."

"Excuse me?"

Father Henry's face hardened. "Your family has split the church far too long. Some of us believe that you should be protected, others believe the Blackwells should be extinct."

"What's that supposed to mean?"

Father Henry rummaged through a drawer of his desk. He stepped up to Nicholas and covered his mouth with a wet cloth. Pressing hard, he spoke, "Forgive me, Father, for I have sinned…"

The fumes rising off the towel filled Nicholas's head, jumbling his thoughts. He felt weak and dizzy. His vision darkened and he fell over.

"It ends with you," Father Henry whispered into Nicholas's ear.

Nicholas felt himself being dragged over the floor, dropped into water. The fountain. The last thing he remembered was the lion and the unicorn, blurring above him as he drifted off into a dark slumber.

Nicholas stood in the middle of a long tunnel. A bright light shone into his face. He shielded his eyes.

His mother's voice echoed in his mind. Warmth coursed through his body. *Turn back, Nicholas. You're not done yet. One more sin remains.*

Nicholas turned away from the light.

*Help me, Nicholas.* It was Amy who spoke, he was sure of it. *It hurts.*

He ran toward the darkness, wondering where the tunnel led. The passage ended abruptly and he fell out, into a valley. *Where am I? Who Am I?* He had completely forgotten his life. Nothing made sense or seemed real, as if he was walking through a dream with amnesia.

He grabbed his inhaler and took a puff. With his lungs relaxed, he started forward. Mounds of broken skeletons rose in his path. Old, tattered human corpses stood around in the fog with bowed heads. He averted his eyes and kept on going. A fire crackled in the distance and he headed toward it. He tried to recall six random objects in his backpack that was slung over his shoulder. Six. He could recall what they were, but not how he obtained them. Or why.

At the end of the valley stood a palace of white stone, surrounded by darkness. A marble phoenix sat above the entrance. A fire blazed in a basin made by the phoenix's wings. Along the stone archway, written in an elegant font, were the words: *Blackwell Manor.*

A bony hand gripped Nicholas's shoulder. He turned and faced a tattered and shriveled body, crippled and frail. Nicholas shivered as he recognized his father. *But why does he look so old and frail?*

"Turn back, Nicholas." Father's weak voice matched his appearance. He tugged Nicholas away from the entrance.

"Dad?" Tears stung his eyes. "How did you get here?"

"He traps..." Wheezing kept him from continuing. He tried again. "He traps us here... All of us..."

"All of who?" Nicholas asked.

Oliver turned and pointed a trembling finger toward the rest of the decaying bodies. "The Blackwell line... All of us men... Trapped in this insanity..."

"Why?" Nicholas gripped his father's hand. He bit his lip, hoping to stop his uncontrollable tremor.

"He wants our family for himself... Refuses to let us go to the light... He forbids us entrance into Heaven." He looked into Nicholas's eyes, his fingers pressed against his crusty lips. "My boy, my little... Nicholas..."

"I thought I forgot what you looked like," Nicholas said.

"You were just a little boy... I've thought of you every second of every day... Your face is the only thing that has kept me from forgetting life... It has kept me from insanity and allowed me to survive my suffering... Only you..." He pressed his hand against Nicholas's cheek. With his other hand, Oliver pulled off an emerald ring from his finger and handed it over to Nicholas.

A tear ran down Nicholas's face as he took his father's ring. "Come with me."

"Nothing would make me so happy... But Nicholas I can't leave... *He* is too strong. You can and you must... Leave this Valley of Death and go through the Tunnel of Light before he claims you, too."

"Dad, he has my friend, Amy. I have to save her."

"Please, Nicholas... Leave... I beg of you... Go to the light... Go to your mother..."

"Mom?"

"Please..." Oliver begged.

"I can't just leave Amy behind. You wouldn't leave mom, I know you wouldn't."

Oliver looked into Nicholas's eyes. "Then you have doomed your soul..." Slowly Oliver Blackwell backed away, stepping into the shadows. Darkness swallowed him.

"Dad!" Nicholas wiped his tears and faced the entrance to the palace. The phoenix's fire rose and sizzled in the basin brighter than before.

His heart thundered in his chest as he entered the palace. Black granite flecked with red covered the floor. Firelight cast dancing shadows against the walls painted with unicorns slaying lions, angels with swords striking one another, the Grim Reaper taking souls. Death. These walls were covered in it.

Nicholas continued through the long hallway. A massive chamber opened at the end. On an ornate throne sat the most handsome man he had ever seen. His features were chiseled to perfection. Gorgeous blue eyes lifted toward Nicholas. In his hands, he held a chain that fell beside his throne and bound Amy by both wrists. She sat at his feet, wearing a white silk dress, her wings disheveled as if from a recent fight.

"Nicholas Blackwell." The man smirked. "Do you know who I am?"

Nicholas stood in the doorway. He wanted to sprint to Amy, but he knew he would be stopped before reaching her. So he waited, slowly walking forward, keeping his distance from the throne.

"Lucifer," he said.

"Very good. And here I thought you not intelligent enough to solve your life's puzzle." He rose, dropping Amy's chains. "I gave you countless clues, evidence, inklings of truth. I even helped you numerous times to get to me. Yet you struggled beyond belief. Honestly, I'm surprised you made it here." He swept toward Amy, slowly circling her.

"Well I have. Now, let Amy go."

Lucifer tossed his head back and laughed, his hand brushing through Amy's auburn hair. "What makes you think you have any authority here? I am the greatest of evils." He pushed Amy to the floor and stepped over her as he crossed the room, toward Nicholas. "I am worshiped by villains, cherished among demons, feared throughout the Mankind's World, yet you, a little orphan boy, think you can throw orders at me?"

"Please."

Lucifer smirked, "Now begging. How truly pathetic you are."

"Take me instead." Nicholas stepped forward.

"Nicholas, no!" Amy shouted.

"Shut up." Lucifer lifted an eyebrow. "Are you insane, Nicholas? You wish to challenge me?"

"Are you scared?"

"Enough of this nonsense. Hand over all of the pieces of *my* Crown." He began circling Nicholas, his beautiful face hardened. "Don't you see? This was all a game. You were to venture through Demonio and challenge my Guardians of Sin to claim my Crown."

"You can't have it," Nicholas said.

"Here's the thing about the Devil's Crown: It truly is an ordinary crown. No enchantments have blessed it, no spells have conquered it. The ability it wields is only the power we believe it to have."

"That doesn't make any sense."

"It makes perfect *sense*," Lucifer hissed. "Risen demons grovel to my Crown, angels desire it, demons worship it, and the Mankind's World would fall to it. All of us, every one of us, long for the powers of the Devil's Crown; when truly it is our desire for the Crown that gives it the power. And you, Nicholas, were the one to bring it here."

"Why me?"

"Because no one else could have survived. You are the last living human who stood a chance. You never understood how easy my Princes were to defeat." Lucifer folded his arms across his broad chest. "Tell me Nicholas, have you ever wondered why any time you asked a Guardian a question they had no choice but to answer? Why do you think Avarice, my Prince of Greed, was so easily overturned?"

"Because his virtue weakened him," Nicholas answered.

"Your charity did weaken him. However, it didn't force him to answer your questions."

Nicholas remembered how Avarice spoke, struggling, as if the words were forced out of him by an invisible power. How the leprechaun had forced his piece of the Crown into Nicholas's blooded hand, rather than continue divulging the secrets he obviously didn't want to reveal.

"Then why did he?" Nicholas asked.

"You are a counselor of demons. My subjects, my Princes for that matter, have no choice but to obey your commands. All because of your heritage." Lucifer's eyes locked with Nicholas. "You still don't know, do you?" he smirked. "The Blackwell family secret?"

"What are you talking about?"

Lucifer smiled and put his lips to Nicholas's ear. "A secret that could change the world."

Nicholas waited, willing himself not to show how much he wanted for Lucifer to continue.

"Do you know how I originally fell from Heaven?" Lucifer said.

"You fell in love with Inanna."

At the mention of the Phoenix's name, Lucifer's face softened. He looked perplexed as Nicholas said, "Which was not allowed. Love was much too overpowering and corrupted you. Not to mention you wanted to be God and that you fashioned the first sin, pride."

"The final Guardian." Lucifer smiled.

"I know it's you. The Guardian of Pride. The last Prince of Hell."

Lucifer laughed. "I'm no Prince, I'm a *king*, you fool." He grabbed Nicholas by the collar of his shirt and forced him closer. "As the story goes, I defied my father and refused my wings of grace. I lived in the Mankind's World as one of them.

I adopted a last name and was married… Do you know why Inanna betrayed me?"

"She saw the Enchanted, suffering."

"She looked upon the eyes of innocence. A child. Our baby boy."

"I feel so bad for you," Nicholas mocked. "But what does your history have to do with my family's secret?"

Lucifer grinned. "The last name I adopted was Blackwell."

Nicholas stepped back, feeling as if the floor had just been kicked from under his feet.

"I don't believe you," he whispered.

Lucifer laughed. "Of course you do. Think about it. Why do you think you hold power over my Princes? Why do you think you connect so easily which each sin? Not only are you the descendent of the greatest evil to have ever existed, but you, in fact, are the last Guardian of Sin. The Pride."

"No! That can't be."

"Afraid so, little boy. The Blackwell men have always been proud, infamous seekers, counselors of demons, charmers who had it all: good looks, riches, fame. Every one of you was the Guardian of Pride, one of seven great Princes of Hell. The moment your father handed over his piece of the Crown, right outside the doors of this palace, you became my last Guardian." Lucifer ran his fingers through his black hair. "The demons that killed your parents were not there to kill you. They were there to give the Crown to you.

"Now, tell me, Nicholas." Lucifer glanced at Nicholas's backpack, and it shredded. The six pieces of the Crown lifted and circled Lucifer, dancing in the air. "Comb of Lust, Goblet of Gluttony, Hand of Greed, Wand of Sloth, Blade of Wrath, Pearl of Envy. What will be your piece of the Devil's Crown, Nicholas Blackwell?"

Nicholas reached into his pocket for his father's ring.

The silver began dripping, slowly morphing into a hand mirror.

"The last piece of the Devil's Crown. My Crown." Lucifer stood behind Nicholas, hands pressed gently against his shoulders. "Look into the mirror."

Nicholas looked. In the mirror, he didn't wear his school uniform, but a mauve tunic. A majestic silver crown embedded with colored jewels sat upon his head. The Devil's Crown, he realized, each of its seven jewels representing its corresponding sin.

"You, Nicholas Blackwell, are my Prince, the greatest of them all. The strongest, most seductive sin. You are my last Guardian. Stand beside your first father and help me rule this underworld."

Nicholas hesitated. He could be a ruler. He was sure he had been made for greatness, not to spend his days as an orphan boy stuck at St. Christopher's Academy. Images floated through his head, of power, glory, all the things he should have been and could yet be.

Then he looked at Amy, watching him with wide eyes. He met her gaze, realizing with sudden clarity what he needed to do.

He turned to Lucifer. "In school, Amy told us a story of the fall of the first angel. The archangels weakened Lucifer with a sword that was said to be forged out of the blood of Lucifer's betrayal and the tears of God's sorrow." Nicholas reached for the Sword of Michael drifting around Lucifer's head with the rest of the Crown pieces. "This sword is your weakness."

Wings rose from Lucifer's back, long and leathery, as black as his hair. "Do not attempt to threaten me. I own all you Blackwell men. You are *my* Sons of Darkness. Either stand beside me or die by my hand."

"I will never stand beside you," Nicholas said.

Lucifer's eyes narrowed. "You will bow to me, my son. Kneel."

"Never."

Lucifer seized Nicholas's shoulder and forced him down

to his knees. "Bow, you ingrate. Bow!"

"Pugdush not let King of Darkness harm Nicholas!"

Lucifer turned. There in the doorway stood Pugdush, arms folded across his furry chest. Dozens of Risen demons crowded beside him, including Ramiro, Master Thril and Master Ling. Beasts and fairies flooded in. A troll with a dumb look on his face stumbled out of the corridor at a slouch and rose to its full height. Demented elves scurried beside Pugdush, fists raised.

"You must be joking." Lucifer paused for a moment, taking in the unbelievable sight. "How dare you betray me." His roar blasted off the roof, cracking the stone structure. The ceiling caved in. Whirlwinds caught the fairies, sweeping them up into the black sky.

Nicholas darted to Amy. With the Sword of Michael, he sliced through her chains.

Her eyes teared. "I'm so sorry, Nicholas."

He pulled her into a hug. "I thought… you might be… gone. What happened to your stab wound?"

She smiled. "Angels heal fast."

A swirl of white lights appeared beside them and morphed into Gabriel, his wings raised. He turned to Lucifer, shielding Nicholas and Amy.

"Stop this madness, brother," Gabriel said.

Lucifer chuckled, rubbing his hands together. "Well, look who came to join in on the fun."

Nicholas tossed Gabriel the sword.

Lucifer held out his hand and fire whirled against his palm, leaving behind the hilt of a sword, a blade forming off it, stretching to its full length. The weapons clashed.

Amy clenched Nicholas's hand, watching the fight. "I'm sorry, Nicholas, I didn't want to lie to you. I just had to keep it from you. Until Lucifer stabbed me I was able to block your sight from ever seeing my wings."

Nicholas shrugged. "I get it. You're an angel. No big deal."

"No, Nicholas. That was just part of the secret."

"Part of it?"

"I am your guardian angel." Her lips trembled as if she was about to cry.

Nicholas frowned. Guardian angel. He supposed it made sense, the way she always stood by his side, the way she tried to guide and protect him even when it meant risking her life. But why was she so sad about it?

"The day I died," Amy said, "I was reborn into a chosen angel, hand-picked by Gabriel. He appeared before me himself, the moment my life slipped away. He needed an apprentice to replace Lucifer who had been trained by Gabriel to become an eighth archangel before he turned away from the Light. I don't know why, but Gabriel selected me as his next apprentice. He taught me everything I know. And you… You were my last test."

"Your last *test?*" Nicholas's frown deepened. He didn't feel he could possibly handle any more secrets.

Amy nodded. "The final challenge before I become an archangel was to become a guardian angel to a little boy who would need more guidance than any other. "

"More guidance?" Nicholas smiled. "I suppose I do. And you've been great at it. But… isn't it a good thing? It means you can stay with me all the time, doesn't it? Even though having an angel for a girlfriend would be hard to explain back home."

She shook her head, her eyes once again pooling with tears. "Guardian angels are not allowed to reveal themselves, or else we would lose the human we are guarding. I didn't tell you who I was because I didn't want to lose you."

Nicholas looked into her green eyes. He gently ran his hand through her red curls, tossed by the violent wind above them. "It was you that night. The night my parents were murdered.

A little girl with red hair saved me from the demons. That girl was you, wasn't it?"

Amy nodded. "When a child is born, their guardian angel becomes that same age, so that the human and the angel can grow up together."

Clashing from the fight in the center of the hall drew their attention. Nicholas frowned. How could they possibly forget the battle going on beside them?

Lucifer swung his sword wide, slashing into Gabriel's side. The wound quickly healed itself, but blisters now covered Gabriel's skin around the wound, similar to those that appeared on Amy's hand when she used Socordia's wand.

Lucifer lifted his sword above him and thrust downward. Gabriel blocked the attack and swung out. The weapons continued to clash as the fight went on.

Nicholas spotted the pieces of the Devil's Crown laying scattered on the floor. It would be difficult to collect them with Gabriel and Lucifer dancing between them, but could he do it? He judged the distance, ready to dive for the nearest piece, when Pugdush appeared at his side.

"Pugdush help."

"Thanks, buddy," Nicholas smiled.

The little Risen demon hurried to collect all the pieces of the Devil's Crown. He grabbed the ruby-speckled comb and the silver goblet and tossed both pieces to Nicholas. Avoiding Lucifer's stomping feet, he leapt and rolled, scurrying under Gabriel's legs toward Avarice's Hand of Greed. Tossing it to Nicholas, he grabbed his mother's Wand of Sloth, then the black pearl and Nicholas's hand mirror. Nicholas grabbed the pieces and handed them to Amy, who made a circle out of them, so that each piece barely touched the other.

The Crown was nearly complete. All they needed was the Sword of Michael.

As if sensing these thoughts, Gabriel glanced in their direction and threw his sword to Pugdush. The Risen demon jumped and caught the sword by the handle, sinking from the weight of the powerful blade. He smiled as he handed the weapon to Nicholas.

Nicholas placed the Sword into the Crown, connecting the pieces to complete the circle. Words tingled on his lips, unknown words coming out on their own, as if eager to be spoken.

"*Vocans diaboli coronam.*"

The seven pieces melted and morphed together into the silver crown Nicholas had seen himself wearing when he had looked into his Mirror of Pride.

Before he could pick up the Crown, Lucifer swung his sword, aiming at Nicholas's heart. Pugdush sprung in front of Nicholas, blocking the attack. The dark blade sank into his tiny chest.

"Pugdush!" Nicholas screamed.

"No!" Amy cried.

Lucifer yanked his blade out from Pugdush's chest and stepped back, watching them with a smug expression.

Nicholas rushed to his tiny friend and scooped him into his arms. Pugdush's breath was labored, his round eyes unfocused as life seeped out of them. His fur was soaked with dark, sticky blood.

"What a fool," Lucifer said.

Blood rushed into Nicholas's face. Carefully, he handed Pugdush's limp body to Amy, then picked up the Devil's Crown and placed it on his head.

Power surged through him. He felt invincible, force tingling at his fingers, ready to fulfill his every command. He imagined a sword in his hand and it appeared. He tightened his grip around the hilt as he stepped toward Lucifer.

"Hand over my Crown," Lucifer said.

Fire flared tall in the stone basin near Lucifer's throne. An enormous bird with ruby and golden feathers rose from the flames. Fire seared the granite floor as the bird landed between Nicholas and Lucifer.

"Inanna," Lucifer said softly, looking into the bird's eyes.

The bird's curved beak did not move as she spoke, her voice filling the room as if she communicated directly from her mind. "This child is not just your descendent, Lucifer, but mine as well."

Nicholas froze. Behind him, he could hear Gabriel and Amy ushering everyone out into the hallway.

"Nicholas, come on!" Amy shouted.

Nicholas shook his head. He stood behind the Phoenix, unable to draw his eyes away. Even as a bird she looked beautiful, her crimson eyes glowing with ageless wisdom, fire drawing ornaments over her golden feathers.

Lucifer was looking at her too. A black tear rolled down his face.

"I've thought of you every day," he said quietly.

"Have you thought of the pain you caused?" The Phoenix shook her head. "You think our family stands in Darkness, when I know they are of Light. You shall never cause them harm again." She raised her wings and erupted into flames. A blast of fire engulfed the room, tearing down the walls. Nicholas felt the heat on his face, but strangely he did not feel hurt. Perhaps the Devil's Crown he still wore was protecting him?

Amy cradled Pugdush's lifeless body in her arms as hastily Gabriel ushered the Risen demons out of the palace into the Valley of Death. The building behind them exploded, collapsing as they ran out. Amy turned back to the blast, momentarily deaf.

"Nicholas!" she cried.

Gently, she put Pugdush down on a flat stone and moved to rush back into the flames, but Gabriel held her back. She struggled uselessly, then collapsed against his chest, her tears drenching Gabriel's shirt.

The flames died down as quickly as they started, leaving behind nothing but ruin and piles of gray ash. With renewed strength, Amy pulled out of Gabriel's grasp and ran.

"Amy, no!" he yelled after her.

Amy ignored him as she hurried through the field of ash that used to be the hallway leading to the throne room.

"Nicholas!" she screamed frantically, searching through the surroundings.

A pile of ash ahead of her stirred and a naked man rose to his feet. His once-black hair and pale skin now looked uniformly gray. He was wearing the Devil's Crown.

"Nicholas?" Amy whispered in disbelief.

Ramiro ran up to her, blinking.

"The Phoenix will rise from its ashes," he rasped.

All the Risen demons around them were dropping to their knees, heads bowing. Ramiro snapped his fingers and a cloak materialized in his hands. He stepped forward and wrapped it around Nicholas.

Amy rushed to Nicholas and pulled him into a hug.

Nicholas hid his face in her hair, cradling her.

"Nothing could keep me from you," he whispered. "Not even the Devil."

Gabriel approached them.

"Can you help Pugdush?" Nicholas asked.

The archangel shook his head. "I'm sorry. There was nothing I could do. I can only heal the Good. No demons, not even if they're as good as Pugdush."

Nicholas nodded again, his eyes trailing to where Pugdush's little body lay on a flat stone.

"Rest in peace, my friend."

"Let's go home." Gabriel spread his wings. A flurry of feathers spun around them, pulling them into a twirl, and they disappeared from the Valley of Death.

# THE NEW
# PRINCIPAL

Å warm day dawned at St. Christopher's Academy. Sun rays beamed into Nicholas's bedroom window, shining onto his face. He rubbed his eyes and sat up in bed, leaning against his headboard. His eyes slid over Dexter sitting on his nightstand. For a moment a vision of his father in the Valley of Death seared his memory. He jumped out of bed, his bare feet instantly cold on the floor.

"You alright?"

Nicholas turned around to see Theodore carrying a stack of textbooks. He smiled. He had never imagined he could feel so happy to see his clumsy nerd of a roommate.

"Hey, Theodore."

"Where have you been? You've been gone for a week. And then you slept for almost two whole days straight."

Nicholas rubbed his forehead. He remembered everything that happened to him in Demonio, but it all seemed distant, like a dream. A week, eh? It seemed more like a lifetime. Could it be that he really dreamed it all?

"It's a long story," he said.

Theodore shook his head. "You're acting strange." He tossed his stack of books on his bed. "Are you sure you are all right?"

Nicholas took a breath. Was he sure?

"I think so," he said.

Theodore shrugged. "Well, you've missed a lot. Members of the Vatican came to school a couple days ago. They took Father Henry back to Rome. I don't think he wanted to go. They said he was getting an early retirement, but I suspect he must have done something bad. Anyway, I don't think anyone here would really miss him."

Nicholas nodded. He surely wouldn't miss Father Henry. Not after the principal tried to kill him. Or did he dream that too?

"It was all pretty exciting," Theodore went on. "The Pope was even here! And you wouldn't believe who he appointed as new principal!"

"Who?"

"Gabriel, the school janitor."

"Gabriel?" Nicholas's eyes widened.

"Yup. It turns out he actually is a priest or something. Oh, and Nicholas, since you are finally awake you might want to go see Amy. She's been stopping by almost every hour to check up on you."

Nicholas jumped to his feet. "Amy? Where is she?"

"Last thing she told me was that she was going to go for a walk to the front gate. She wanted some fresh air."

Without another word, Nicholas quickly jumped up and raced out of the room. He darted down the hall, passing by students and nuns. Down the stairs to the first floor. Out of the door, sprinting through the field. The wet grass, the fresh cool breeze, the sun, never felt as good as it did right now. He felt the familiar burning in his lungs, but even that felt good. Nicholas knew he would need his inhaler soon, but he didn't care. He was alive. Amy was waiting.

She stood right outside the half-opened gate. Even the plain school uniform couldn't mask her beauty. Her auburn hair fell over her shoulders in silky waves. Her green eyes glistened, a smile tugging at the corners of her mouth.

Nicholas ran up to her and pulled her into his arms.

"Where are your wings?" he asked.

She smiled. "Now that it's over I can hide them again." She heaved a deep sigh, looking into his eyes. "I'm so proud of you."

"You mean, you don't mind that I'm a direct descendant of pure evil?"

Amy shook her head. "You are a hero."

A hero. He liked the sound of that. But somehow, all the things that this title encompassed—fame, admiration, worship—didn't seem so important anymore. He felt a different form of excitement as he looked at Amy, so close, so beautiful. His fingers brushed her cheek as he looked deep into her eyes, feeling happy like never before. "I didn't realize how much I loved you until I almost lost you."

Amy's gaze wavered. "Nicholas, they won't let us be together. It's forbidden. I am only here to say goodbye."

"Do you love me?"

She held his gaze. "Yes."

Yes. He felt his head spin. "Then nothing else matters, does it?"

She shook her head. "If Gabriel, or the others, found out we were together, you would be taken away from me. Regardless of any feelings we might have for each other, I shouldn't even be your angel anymore because you know what I am. Gabriel has agreed to make an exception this time, but…we're not supposed to love each other the way we want to. Remember, this all started because of an angel's forbidden love."

"I don't care." Nicholas took Amy's hand, feeling her shiver at his touch. "I can't imagine not seeing you. Amy. I would face

Demonio and all the Guardians of Sin again just to be with you. I can't lose you."

A smile lit up Amy's face. "You're not losing me. I've been with you ever since you were born. Any time you felt good for no reason, a sudden warmth, that was me standing over you. Guiding you. Protecting you. I will continue to do it. I might be leaving, but I'm not going anywhere." She pulled away and stepped back, putting distance between them.

A tear rolled down Nicholas's cheek. He stood still for a moment, then ran after her, grabbed her shoulders, and pulled her into a kiss.

It felt as though time had slowed and their kiss lasted for hours, when truly it was only a moment. Their lips pulled apart and again Amy took a step back, looking at him with longing.

"No matter what, I love you, Amy. I will always love you."

"We will find a way," she whispered. A white light engulfed her and she disappeared. A ribbon of brilliantly white feathers swirled up into the sky, climbing higher and higher before vanishing.

After a long while, Nicholas turned and faced the gate. The gargoyle statues were staring down at him. One of them looked new and had an uncanny resemblance to an old friend… *Pugdush?* He smiled as he stepped toward the statue.

Suddenly he knew exactly what to do. He was, after all, a Prince of Hell.

"Pugdush awaken," he ordered.

The stone cracked, sending tiny fissures across the crust. The gargoyle shattered and Pugdush shook the remaining stone off his body. He looked at Nicholas with round, wet eyes, then jumped into his arms.

"Pugdush so happy to see Nicholas is well."

"Me, too." Nicholas laughed for the first time in a very long time. "What happened to you? I thought you were dead."

"Pugdush has become truly Risen. To be a gargoyle, is the first step of penance for a Risen demon. Sacrifice to save greater good made Pugdush worthy of Light. Pugdush can now be in sunlight." The little demon closed his eyes and shivered with pleasure as the sunshine slid against his fur.

"That's great, Pugdush. And… thanks for saving my life back there. I wouldn't be here if it wasn't for you."

"Pugdush love Nicholas."

"I love you too, buddy."

A flurry of white feathers floated down and pushed the iron gates open. Nicholas felt a sudden warmth as he stood up.

"Gabriel is waiting for you," Pugdush said. "Pugdush now must protect St. Christopher's Academy and his best friend."

"Thanks." Nicholas hesitated. "Um. Can gargoyles eat chocolate?"

"Chocolate?" Pugdush's eyes lit up.

"I'll make sure to bring you some, every day."

"You would do that for Pugdush? Really?"

Nicholas laughed. "I promised, remember? When you shrank us back in Demonio to help us into the sewer? All the chocolate you want."

"Yum!" Pugdush jumped happily, then took his post beside the gate and his body instantly hardened into stone.

Nicholas followed the stream of feathers back to school. He opened the front door and entered the hall that was filled with crowds of students. For a moment he headed toward the janitor's room, but quickly changed direction and headed to the principal's office. Normally, he dreaded this route, but now it didn't bother him at all.

He pushed the door open. Gabriel stood with his back turned, looking out of the massive window into the sky. He slowly turned and faced Nicholas with a welcoming smile.

"So, how does a former janitor, who actually is an archangel, become a principal?" Nicholas asked.

Gabriel's smile widened. "Well, Nicholas, St. Christopher's Academy has more secrets than it might seem. Let's just say these secrets need a really good protector."

"So, Principal Gabriel. It has a nice ring to it. Does this mean I can get away with more mischief than usual?"

Gabriel laughed. "Not at all. On the contrary, I'm going to have to watch you more closely. Nicholas, you must be very careful now. Demons are going to know the fall of the seven Princes of Hell was by your hand. Lucifer will send his servants after you as he did for your parents. The only place where you can be protected is here at the Academy."

"But, we killed Lucifer. Or at least the Phoenix did."

"No. Inanna just trapped him once again within the walls of Hell. But my brother has many ways of resurfacing. He won't stop until the final war ends."

Nicholas lowered his head. "You mean, everything Amy and I did in Demonio was for nothing?"

"Not at all." Gabriel circled his desk, putting his hand on Nicholas's shoulder. "Because of you, seven Princes have fallen. You and Amy will not be forgotten in Demonio. You fought the seven Guardians of Sin and trapped each one of them in their piece of the Crown. Risen demons now honor you, angels respect you, demons fear you. I'd say you did very well."

Nicholas smiled.

"Nicholas, your father would be very proud. You see, though many Blackwells have fought the Guardians and trapped them throughout history, none of them had conquered all seven sins."

"I thought my parents did?"

Gabriel shook his head. "Oliver Blackwell was a good man, but there was one sin that even he had never defeated. His own Pride. This was why he carried his piece of the Devil's Crown until the day he died. Like you've discovered along your journey,

Pride is the most powerful of sins and the most difficult one to overcome. When you fought to rescue Amy, putting her needs above your own, you defeated it. Thus, you became the one and only true champion of sin."

Nicholas nodded. Strange how even after these words he didn't feel any pride. Did he truly defeat it, even in his own heart?

"What happened to the Devil's Crown?" he asked.

"It was separated once again into its seven pieces and they are now well protected."

"So, what happens now?"

Gabriel's smile became gentle. "Why don't you go have some fun? Go see your friends. Have a meal. Enjoy today for all it is."

Nicholas nodded. He wanted to ask the archangel about Amy. He didn't think he could truly enjoy any day knowing he would never see her again. But he knew there was probably nothing he could do. It was useless even to talk about it.

"Thanks, Gabriel," he said. "For everything."

He left the room and headed to the school pool. He didn't know how he was going to get back into his old life, interact with his friends, head the swim team, now that Amy was gone and he didn't know if he would ever see her again. Compared to that, even knowing that demons existed and would soon come after him did not seem as significant.

Gabriel looked out the window, listening to the trickling of the fountain. In all the centuries he had lived, in all the jobs his father had appointed him to, he had never had to be a principal of an actual school. Perhaps this would be his greatest test. There was so much to worry about, with darkness on the horizon.

A light swirled between the front door and the fountain.

As the lights subsided, there stood Amy.

"Hello, Gabriel." She sounded sad.

"Hello, Amy." He looked at her. "I must say, you were amazing. You surely have the makings of a great archangel."

"Thank you." Her smile did not touch her eyes as she continued to watch him.

"You did everything I asked of you, flawlessly. Enrolled in St. Christopher's Academy. Befriended Nicholas. Framed him by pouring soap into the school pool. Found the Great Serpent and allowed him into the school grounds. Journeyed through Demonio to take on the Guardians of Sin. You did far more than expected. I'm very proud of you." Gabriel hesitated. "Though I must say, I was surprised at your outburst of emotion when you thought Nicholas was dead. That looked much more than the love of an angel to a human."

Amy blushed. "It's taken care of."

"Is it?"

She lowered her eyes.

Gabriel sighed. "My last apprentice left me scarred. It took many centuries to get over Lucifer's betrayal. I can't bear another. Which is why I will offer you a choice. One that has never been granted to any angel before you."

Amy lifted her head. Gabriel's heart quivered at the hope he saw in her eyes. "A choice?"

"One you will not make today, but later on, when you're truly capable to make this decision." Gabriel held her gaze. "I will allow you and Nicholas to see each other."

"You will?"

"No more than once a month."

Amy's smile faded quickly under Gabriel's stern look.

"I am giving you this time to decide if Nicholas's love is worth clipping your wings," Gabriel said. "When the moment comes, you must choose."

"Choose?" she swallowed.

Gabriel nodded. "If you choose Nicholas, you will become human. You will live out your days like a regular mortal. While you may still become an angel after you die—if you are worthy—you will no longer be offered a chance to become the eighth archangel."

Amy's smile lit up her face, so happy that Gabriel couldn't help but smile in return. He was losing a promising archangel, he knew. But sometimes these things were just worth it.

"Thank you!" Amy hugged him, then turned and ran out of the office.

Standing at the window, Gabriel saw her emerge from the building downstairs, and run toward Nicholas walking through the grounds down to the pool.

"Nicholas!" she shouted. "Nicholas!"

Nicholas turned, just as she jumped into his arms and kissed him.

Gabriel watch them talking, then kissing, then talking again. He turned away, glancing over the Academy grounds. Then he stepped back to his desk.

He was a school principal now, and he had work to do.

# THE END

# ABOUT THE AUTHOR

Jonathan L. Ferrara was born in San Pedro, California to an Italian fisherman and a mother from New York. Growing up with one older brother, Jonathan had several hobbies: finding the best hiding spots to jump out and scare his mother, discovering new fantasy book series, and imagining outrageous, whimsical worlds full of magic. He is now happily married, residing in California in the City of Angels. He has two wonderful children—his dog Koda and cat Merlin.

His author's website is www.JonathanLFerrara.com

# More from Dragonwell Publishing:

**Mistress of the Solstice**
by Anna Kashina

a dark romantic tale
based on Russian
folklore

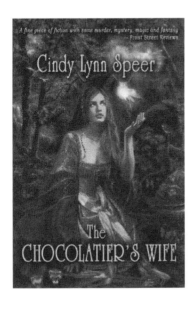

**The Chocolatier's Wife**
by Cindy Lynn Speer

a rich tale of romance,
magic, mystery
...and chocolate

# More from Dragonwell Publishing:

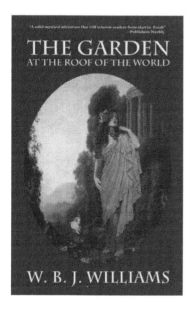

**The Garden at the Roof of the World**
by W. B. J. Williams

a medieval quest
of healing, magic, and
love

**Lex Talionis**
by R. S. A. Garcia

"A stunning debut"
—*Publishers Weekly*

# More from Dragonwell Publishing:

**Once Upon a Curse**
by Peter Beagle
and other authors

the dark side
of fairy tales and myths

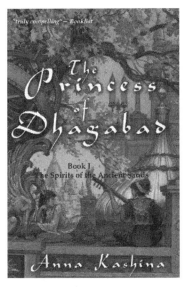

**The Princess of
Dhagabad**
by Anna Kashina

an Arabian love story
about a princess
and an all-powerful djinn

Made in the USA
Coppell, TX
02 July 2020

29874747R00134